## AN AVALON MYSTERY

## A DEADLY CHANGE OF HEART
### A Devonie Lace Mystery
Gina Cresse

Devonie has a knack for stumbling into trouble. After she successfully bids on a Ford Explorer at a U.S. Marshal's auction, she finds she's bought more than just an SUV. The surprise "extra" lands her in the middle of a police investigation into the death of a local reporter.

Unsatisfied with the detective's conclusion that the death was an accident, Devonie sets out to find the killer on her own. Her efforts to retrace the reporter's steps as she worked on her last story gives Devonie a number of clues, and just as many suspects. The dead woman's estranged husband keeps landing at the top of Devonie's list, but stolen plutonium, homemade atomic bombs, and a shady drug dealer add other possibilities to her growing list of suspects.

When Devonie gets too close to discovering the identity of the murderer, she becomes the next target of a killer who'll stop at nothing to protect his interests.

# A DEADLY CHANGE OF HEART

•

## GINA CRESSE

*AVALON BOOKS*
NEW YORK

PRINTED IN THE UNITED STATES OF AMERICA
ON ACID-FREE PAPER
BY HADDON CRAFTSMEN, BLOOMSBURG, PENNSYLVANIA

This is for Rose and Larry, AKA Mom and Dad.

## Chapter One

Diane Parker slipped her sunglasses into a hard plastic case as she stepped through the glass doors into the reception area of her husband's office. She stopped momentarily and stared at the collection of greasy handprints on the usually sparkling glass displaying the name of Bradley Parker's first love: Business Solutions, Inc.—or BS Inc., as Diane liked to call it. The mauve carpet showed a grease stain in the shape of a shoe where a thoughtless delivery person failed to use the mat outside before tracking in the oily mess. Diane noticed droppings from the paper hole punch scattered on the floor. She ran her finger along the counter and drew a long, thin line in the dust. She gazed around the small reception area as she wiped the dust off her finger on a tissue she retrieved from Cathy's vacant desk. The place looked deserted.

"Cathy?" she called as she straightened the pile of old magazines scattered across the heavy oak coffee table in the corner.

"Be right there," a man's voice called from another room.

Diane searched for a wastepaper basket to toss her dusty tissue away. Bradley Parker emerged from his office and saw Diane with her back toward him. "Can I help you?" he asked.

Diane spun around in her dark burgundy pumps and nearly lost her balance. She was on her way to work, and today was the first time she'd worn the new shoes—the dress, too. The dusty-rose–colored knit sweater dress fit snugly in all the right places. She bought it nearly three weeks ago, but purposely waited to wear it until she knew she'd be seeing Bradley—or rather, Bradley would be seeing her. It was the first time in eighteen years she could fit into a size eight and look this good. She finally gave up plucking the few strands of gray hair as they showed up, and let Marcia down at the Visible Changes Hair Salon work her magic. The office fluorescent lights shone on her auburn highlights as Diane pulled a strand of hair away from her face. She smiled at Bradley.

"Oh, it's you!" he said, amazed at the sight in front of him.

"Yeah, it's me. I can't stay long. I'm on my way to work."

Bradley gawked at the beauty standing in the middle of the room. He couldn't remember the last time a woman turned his head the way she just had—not even when he proposed to her so many years ago. His eyes moved down her long, thin neck to the curve of her hips, then continued down the slender legs to her perfect ankles. A dimple appeared in Diane's right cheek as she tried to suppress the smile she felt emerging from within. He just might be feeling something—maybe desire, maybe love, maybe regret.

She cleared her throat and initiated some conversation—any conversation. "Where's Cathy?" she asked.

The question didn't register in Bradley's brain. He was too preoccupied wondering how this woman could have emerged from the frumpy, overweight housewife who'd had the nerve to leave him nearly thirteen months earlier.

Diane strolled over to the empty reception desk. "She does still work here, doesn't she?"

The fog finally cleared in Bradley's head. "Cathy? Uh, yeah . . . sure." He checked his watch. "She's just late today—dentist appointment or something."

Diane grimaced as she noticed a dusty smudge on her sleeve and proceeded to brush it off. "What's up with the cleaning people? They go on strike? This place is a mess."

Bradley rushed over to help her clean the spot from her dress. "I'm looking for a new service. They weren't doing a very good job, so I . . . well, it's not important. What are you doing here?"

Diane stepped back from Bradley. "We need to talk about our . . . about the—"

Bradley stopped her before she could get the D-word out. She hadn't actually said anything about a divorce yet, but he knew it was the next logical step if a reconciliation didn't look promising. "Let's go in my office. We can sit down. You want coffee?"

Diane frowned as she checked her watch. "I really can't stay that long. I told Garrett I'd be a little late, but I don't think he'd appreciate me showing up in time for lunch."

Diane followed Bradley down the hall to his office. He opened the door for her and breathed in the scent of her freesia body lotion as she passed. "Why? All you're doing is filing. They could hire a monkey to do that."

Diane stopped in her tracks, clenched her teeth, and turned on her heel. She glared at him through deep blue eyes—the daggers could have dropped him where he stood. In the past, his dehumanizing comments would have had her in tears in a matter of seconds. Usually, he'd start counting out loud to see if he could break his record. Ten seconds was his best, so far. Diane would not give him the satisfaction. She took a deep breath and caught her reflection in the mirror behind Bradley. She was reminded how much she'd accomplished in the last year, driven by pure anger. She had lost forty pounds—weight she could not diet and exercise away in nineteen years of marriage. She'd found a job that she really loved—one that gave her a sense of self-worth. She no longer felt lost. She didn't wake up every morning and wonder why she existed anymore. She had direction in her life. She felt good. She tried to remember the last time she'd felt this good. Finally, she concluded that she felt better than she ever had in her entire life—too good to let this cold man get the best of her. "Well, they didn't hire a monkey to do the job. Unfortunately, the San Diego Zoo couldn't part with any, so they're stuck with me."

Bradley let out an uneasy chuckle. Humor was not Diane's usual response. He waited for her chin to quiver, but it never happened.

"But they did have the sense to realize a high school kid with a basic grasp of the alphabet could file just as well as I could, for a lot less money," Diane continued.

Bradley smirked. "So you got replaced by a punk kid?"

Diane's lower lip protruded in a pout as she nodded her head.

Bradley grinned. "Maybe you could help out here, at least until—"

"They didn't replace me, Bradley. They promoted me. Remember that bachelor's degree you told me was such a waste of time? Well, the San Diego *Union Tribune* doesn't see a journalism degree as a waste at all. In fact, they think it might just come in handy for their newest reporter."

Bradley choked on her words. "Reporter? You've got to be kidding. You can barely follow the plot of a Saturday-morning cartoon."

His words, which were meant to cut her down, only succeeded in fueling her fire. She took a deep breath and closed her eyes. She struggled to keep her voice calm. "I didn't come here to fight with you, Bradley." She took a step closer to him—a move he wasn't accustomed to. Usually, she tried to keep her distance from him when they argued. Once again, he was distracted by the freesia scent as it wafted around his head.

"Well then, why are you here, Mrs. *Union Tribune* Reporter?" The sarcasm dripped from his lips.

Diane pulled an envelope from her purse and handed it to Bradley. "I filed for divorce. If you have any questions, you can call my attorney."

Bradley's chin hit the floor. He stared at the papers in his hand as though they were the gun that had just fired a bullet into his chest. "Divorce? Diane, can't we talk about this?"

"I tried to talk to you about it. Remember? I couldn't hold your attention long enough to discuss the weather, let alone our marriage. What was her name? Clarissa?"

"Is that what this is all about? Because that's been over for a long time. I swear—"

"And before that, Cheryl. Oh, and let's not forget Tanya."

"Come on, Diane." Bradley moaned, as if he were listening to a broken record.

"It's not just about the affairs, Bradley. I realize I let myself go in the years we were married. I didn't make much of an effort to be attractive for you. But you made me feel like I was nothing—and I'm not nothing. I'm something, Bradley—something special."

"Special? You mean like a princess or a queen? Give me a break, and while you're at it, why don't you grow up. You couldn't have picked a worse time to become *special.* I can't afford to . . . business is not . . . I mean—no. No, we won't do this. Just forget it, Diane." Tiny beads of sweat formed on Bradley's forehead. He tossed the envelope on the floor, like an angry, spoiled child throwing a tantrum.

"Sorry, Bradley, but my attorney assures me that 'I don't want to' won't be an option available to you." Diane stood her ground. For the first time in her life, she was in the offensive rather than defensive position.

Bradley trudged to his desk and sat behind it, resting his forehead in his palms. He could see his usual tactics weren't effective against this new Diane. She wasn't going to be bullied. He remembered how compassionate and soft-hearted she could be, especially with their two sons when they came to her with their problems. He used to criticize her and say she was making mama's boys out of them, but at the moment, that quality could work in his favor. "I can't take this now. Cathy isn't at the dentist. I had to let her go, along with Mark and Tom. The cleaning people, too. I couldn't make the payroll. I'm being sued by three clients."

Diane didn't flinch. She knew what he was up to. She looked him square in the eye and didn't show one emotion—not fear, not hate, not love, and definitely not sympathy.

Bradley felt as though his skin was transparent, and she could see right through him. He felt a drop of perspiration run down his side from his armpit. He finally came to the realization that he had no control over her anymore. "The business is in trouble, so I'm really not interested in this new discovery of how special you are."

"You never were interested. That's the problem." Diane opened the door to leave. "Look, I don't want your business. You can have it. Everything else will be split fifty-fifty. I've already talked to the boys. They can't believe I waited this long to get away from you. I explained that I had to wait until they were both off to college. I could never leave them with the tyrant who lives in our house."

Bradley glared at her. "You'll fall flat on your face. You're not smart enough to make it on your own. You'll be crawling back on all fours when you can't pay your rent or fill your cupboards with candy bars and potato chips."

Diane smiled, displaying the dimples in her cheeks that so many men found disarming. "In case you hadn't noticed, I don't eat candy bars or potato chips anymore." She turned to leave, then stopped for one last jab. "Oh, by the way, you might want to catch *The Flintstones* Saturday morning. Wilma's gonna throw Fred out on his . . . well, you get the picture. See, and you thought I couldn't follow the plot." The smile left Diane's face. "Yaba-daba-doo, Bradley."

Diane closed the door behind her and slipped quickly out

of the building. She jumped into her car, jammed it into gear, and sped out of the parking lot. She was sobbing as she reached the first stoplight.

The mascara stains were dry by the time Diane arrived at the *Tribune*. She waved at the guard in the security shack as she eased her car into the lot and searched for a place to park. Since she was late, the only spot available was a narrow slot next to Garrett's Humvee, or the Hummer, as he liked to call it. Diane bit her lip as she worked to maneuver her Toyota into the skinny spot. "Don't hit the boss's car," she whispered to herself as she set the brake and opened her door, careful to not bang the shiny black paint job on the glorified Jeep. Garrett stood at the entrance of the brick-and-glass building and watched with amusement as she struggled to squeeze out of her car.

"Don't ding the Hummer," he called to her, grinning.

Diane smiled, but didn't reply. As she got closer, Garrett noticed the dark streaks on her face. His grin turned to a frown. "You okay?" he asked.

Diane nodded and brushed past him into the building, then directly to the ladies' room. She cleaned up her makeup, combed her fingers through her thick hair, and smoothed the wrinkles in her dress. She gave her reflection an approving nod then pushed through the door and headed for her desk. Garrett fell in step behind her, carrying two coffee cups. Diane dropped her purse into a drawer, then collapsed into her chair.

Garrett set the steaming cup of coffee on the desk in front of her. "Here. Thought you could use a little boost. No cream, no sugar, just the way you like it."

Diane smiled at him. "Thanks, Garrett."

Garrett watched and waited as she took a sip of the cof-

fee. "So, I'm sure it's none of my business, but . . . can I
. . . is there anything . . . are you okay?"

Diane nodded. "I'm fine, but thanks for asking."

Garrett pulled a chair up to her desk and sat down directly in front of her. "You can't get rid of me that easily.
I'm just going to sit here until you open up that box full
of trouble you carried in here and lay some of it on me."

Diane took another sip. "How long have I worked here?"

Garrett scratched his chin. "Let's see, about a year, I
guess."

"In all the years I was married to Bradley, he never paid
enough attention to know a simple little thing like how I
take my coffee."

"He's a fool, Diane." Garrett took her hand and gave it
a little squeeze. "I take it you stopped to see him this morning. That's why you had to come in late?"

Diane nodded. "I gave him the divorce papers. He didn't
take it well."

"I wouldn't either, if I were losing something as terrific
as you," Garrett said, still holding on to her hand.

"He's not worried about losing me. He's worried about
losing his business. The divorce is just another headache
he doesn't want to deal with right now." Diane took her
hand back from Garrett and continued drinking her coffee.
Garrett wasn't the first man in the office to wear his heart
on his sleeve in her presence. She was flattered by all the
attention she'd received lately, but Diane had a mission,
and she wasn't about to be distracted by romance.

Garrett pushed his chair back and stood up. He placed a
gentle hand on her shoulder. "I'll leave you alone. If you
feel like talking or anything, you know where I am. Okay,
kiddo?"

"Thanks, Garrett. You've been the greatest boss . . . friend I could ever ask for."

Garrett winked. "Get to work, missy. What do you think this is—Marriage Counseling 101?"

Diane laughed as she watched Garrett stroll back to his office and close himself in behind a wall of glass masked by rows of blinds. She pulled the stack of yesterday afternoon's mail from the basket on her desk and sorted through it. One bulky package slipped out of her hands and landed on the floor. She picked it up and tore it open. It contained a videotape labeled *Science Project*. Diane searched the envelope for a note of explanation, but there was nothing else. It was not addressed to any specific editorial department— just general delivery to the San Diego *Union Tribune*. There was no return address, but the postmark indicated that it was mailed from San Diego. She regarded the tape curiously for a moment, then set it on her desk so she could finish going through her mail. If the conference room wasn't tied up, she'd use the VCR to view the tape later, after lunch, if she had time.

Saturday morning found Diane staring forlornly at the ugly black contraption sitting in the corner of her bedroom. The treadmill could be so boring. She peered out the window at the fog and decided it wasn't too thick to keep her away from Point Loma. Sunset Cliffs was a beautiful place to run, and this early in the morning, only a few pelicans and possibly one or two die-hard surfers would be around. She threw a bottle of water, her ankle weights, and a towel in her sports bag and climbed in her car.

She parked her Toyota in a secluded parking area away from the beaten path. Most of the surfers tried to get the spots as close to the water as possible so they wouldn't have to carry their boards too far in their bare feet. Diane didn't have to compete with anyone for the parking spot she chose. This was a favorite place for her to get away from the world. The trails ran along the coastal cliffs, and the view of the Pacific could be breathtaking, as soon as the fog burned off. She strapped the additional five pounds of weights on her ankles, stretched for a few seconds, then jogged down the path at a steady pace.

She felt good. She'd forced the memory of yesterday's confrontation with Bradley out of her mind. She had a whole new life in front of her—new challenges, new opportunities, new experiences. She felt a twinge of excitement as she thought of the possibilities. She smiled and picked up her pace. She was on her second wind, in more ways than one.

Parts of the path were clear and the view to the ocean unobstructed, while other parts were surrounded by dense growth. Diane headed up a short rise, then around a sharp turn in the path that wove through a thick stand of trees. As she rounded a second turn, she spotted a tall man standing a short distance off the trail. She'd startled him and he spun around to see who was coming down the path. Diane stopped. She squinted at him, slightly irritated. She'd run along this trail many times, and never before had she encountered another human being this early in the morning. This was her private world. How dare he invade her sanctuary? She never told anyone about this place—at least no one she could remember.

"Good morning," Diane said.

He didn't reply. His face was angry. Then Diane noticed the second person, a dark-skinned man in an expensive suit.

She noticed the tall man's enraged expression. *How dare you be mad at me? This is my personal space. I didn't invite you here,* she thought to herself.

The shorter man looked over at his companion. "Is this going to be a problem?"

Diane's eyes moved to the open case sitting on the ground between the men. It was full of cash—bills stacked in thick bundles. Next to the case was an aluminum box with heavy-duty handles riveted on both sides. The box was closed tight and a piece of white tape with red markings was wrapped around it as a seal. Diane returned her stare to the tall man. She put the pieces together in her mind. This was some sort of private transaction—illegal enough to require a secluded meeting place—and dangerous to be a witness to.

"Afraid so," the taller man replied to his associate's question.

Diane listened to the words and tried to make sense of the scene. Her initial reaction was confusion. She shouldn't have felt fearful, but her intuition told her to run. She turned and sprinted down the trail in the direction she'd come. The two men started after her. Diane ran as hard and fast as she could. She wanted to shed the ankle weights, but couldn't stop long enough to pull the Velcro straps off. She felt like she was trying to run through wet cement. She wasn't sure if it was the added weight, or the knowledge of what she'd just witnessed, that caused her heart to race. This section of trail had a lot of switchbacks, but Diane tried to run a straight line to shorten the distance between her and her car.

The shorter man gave up the chase when he snagged his silk jacket on a tree branch. The other man pursued Diane relentlessly. His long legs carried him easily through the brush. Diane glanced back once to see if they were gaining, and stumbled over an exposed tree root. She fell and cried out with pain as the rough ground ripped through the knees of her sweatpants. She yanked the Velcro strap on her right ankle as she sprung to her feet but missed the left one. She made three strides before he leaped through the air and tackled her to the ground.

Diane yelled, but no one was around to hear her screams. The other man arrived at the scene a few seconds later. The two men dragged Diane, kicking and screaming, across the trail toward the ocean. She'd managed to finish the job started by the tree branch and ripped the sleeve completely off the expensive silk jacket. She also landed a well-placed blow to the taller man's shin, but couldn't free herself from their grips.

The men dragged her to the edge of the cliff. Her eyes widened with terror when she realized her fate. The high cliffs dropped sharply to the rocky coast, at least a hundred feet below. The deafening sound of the waves pounding on the rocks drowned out Diane's screams of terror as she tumbled over the edge.

## Chapter Two

I stepped off the bus and gazed at my surroundings. I was still officially in San Diego, but I was close enough to the border to hear the barks from the dogs roaming the streets of Tijuana. The city bus let out a puff of smoke as it pulled away from the curb on its way to the next stop. I watched it rumble down the street and hoped I wouldn't need to use it to get back home. I checked my watch and unfolded the map that gave directions to the auction grounds.

My friend Jason was supposed to give me a ride to the auction this morning. When I told him it was a U.S. Marshal's auction of police-seized vehicles, he retracted his offer. He told me if I came back with some drug dealer's car, he was going to move to another state and leave no forwarding address so I couldn't find him.

I explained to him that this was a great way to get a good deal on a car. The public at large doesn't generally know about these auctions and the competition is usually slim. Also, since drug dealers usually pay cash, it's not likely there will be any liens on the properties being sold. Jason ridiculed my explanation and predicted that with my luck, I'd come home with a bargain BMW and find a skeleton in the trunk. I told him he was acting like a paranoid coward and hung up on him. I wasn't really mad at him, but I was desperate to get my own wheels again. My Jeep had been stolen and the insurance company only gave me seventy-five hundred dollars to replace it. I'd been begging, borrowing, and bussing for the last month, and I'd had enough.

No, Devonie Lace is not a public transportation kind of girl. I need to be independent. If I had lived in the days of the old West, you would never have found me in one of those canvas-covered buckboards, traveling in a wagon train across the country. I'd have to have my own horse and the freedom to ride off whenever the mood struck. I couldn't be bogged down with the heavy burden of the other pioneers' needs and worries and weaknesses.

To top it all off, I had a wedding to plan and not a lot of time to get it done. It's challenging enough keeping appointments with florists, caterers, photographers, dressmakers, and ministers without having to memorize a bus schedule that seems to change on a weekly basis.

A wedding. Now that's an occasion I never thought I'd be a party to. My attitude toward marriage began on my first day of kindergarten, when a little brown-haired boy tattled on me for tearing his naptime towel. Didn't he realize I was infatuated and was only trying to get closer by pulling him toward me? Instead of returning my affection, he ran crying to the teacher. That was my first experience at love, and things went steadily downhill from there.

After more than three decades of failed relationships and

heartbreaks, I met Craig, the man I was scheduled to marry in just a few short weeks. He wasn't like any man I'd ever known. I knew he was a nice guy the night my Aunt Arlene tried to fix me up with him during a dinner party, but when he followed me all the way to Switzerland to save me from some very evil people, I couldn't believe it. Nobody ever even followed me home, let alone halfway around the world.

To be honest, though, at first I was a little worried he was one of the bad guys. I mean, in real life, what man would follow a woman he'd just met all the way to Geneva because he thought her life might be in danger? And what man would risk his own life for that same woman? Only in the movies, right? That's what I thought, too. But Dr. Craig Matthews was just such a man. Since I met him, I hadn't had a single dream about being married to Mel Gibson. I still had the occasional Tom Selleck dream, but what red-blooded American woman wouldn't?

Craig offered to buy me a new car to replace my stolen Jeep, but I wouldn't hear of it. Just because I was getting married didn't mean I could no longer take care of my own needs. I assured him I could get a perfectly suitable vehicle with the insurance money I'd received. I hoped this would be the day I found that suitable vehicle, because any more bus rides, and I might sell out and take him up on his offer.

I wandered around the auction grounds and scoped out the vehicles I thought I'd bid on. Unfortunately, I'd missed most of the preview period and would be bidding blind. I narrowed my list to three SUVs that looked promising: a Jeep Grand Cherokee, like the one stolen from me, only red and a few years newer; a white Toyota Forerunner; and a black Nissan Pathfinder. All three were less than two years old and very clean.

The Jeep went for ten grand. I kept my hopes up for the Toyota, but when the bid got over eight thousand, I headed to the next lot before the gavel struck. I hoped I was the last of the serious SUV buyers, and the Pathfinder would be mine. No such luck. My meager seventy-five hundred dollars wasn't going to buy me a ticket off of the City of San Diego's public transportation system—at least not today.

I trudged toward the gates, studying the schedule in my hand to see when the next bus would arrive to take me back to the marina where I live on my sailboat, the *Plan C*. I stopped for a moment and regarded the next lot to be auctioned—a Ford Explorer. I hadn't noticed it before and it's a wonder why. It was orange—not orange like a pleasant, sunset-sky orange, or even a fashionable burnt orange, but orange like the fruit. The crowd was thin and the bidding was about to start. I almost walked off, leaving it for the other bidders, when the thought of another bus ride home flashed through my mind.

When I was in junior high, I rode the bus to school daily. I remember Harry Fate, an all-around troublemaker, would sit in one of the front rows during the hot months when all the windows in the bus were open. There was no air-conditioning and the only relief from the heat was letting the breeze from the outside air blow in your face. Harry would wait until the bus reached an adequate speed, then spit out the window, looking back to see which poor, unsuspecting kid got a spit bath across his or her face. Everyone hated Harry, but he was tough and mean, and no one ever dared to cross him. I learned to sit on the opposite side of the bus from him. There are a lot of Harrys out there and many of them still ride the bus. I pushed my way through the crowd and raised my hand. "Five thousand!" I called out.

Some joker printed the word SUNKIST with a green marker across the door of my new Explorer while I was inside paying for it. I only had to give sixty-five hundred for it, and I planned to use the rest of the insurance money to have it painted. If the lettering didn't come off, that would motivate me to take care of the color sooner than later. As I pulled through the exit gate, a pair of young men smiled and waved at me. One of them held up a green marker and laughed. I smiled and waved back. "Jerk," slipped through my clenched teeth, but he couldn't hear me through my closed windows.

San Diego freeways are probably the busiest in the world. Bumper-to-bumper and door-to-door, there's not always room to maneuver when time is limited. By the time I saw the two-by-four in the lane I was traveling in, it was too late. I hit it with both front wheels and felt the bump-bump as all four tires rolled over it. The steering got sloppy, and I realized I had at least one, if not more, flat tire. I searched the dash for the emergency flasher button and hit it. Then I signaled my intention to move over to the shoulder. Of course, no one would let me move over. They blasted past as though I didn't exist. Finally, a trucker saw my predicament and flashed his lights at me, showing his intention to let me move in front of him, then off to the shoulder. I waved to him as I pulled off and he flashed his lights again.

Both front tires were flat. I called a towing service. The

tow truck drove right on past me. I waited several minutes until he could circle around. He came up behind me again and pulled off the freeway.

"I didn't stop the first time 'cause I thought you were a Caltrans employee, picking up garbage or something. You know, Caltrans trucks are painted almost that same color," the tow-truck driver informed me.

I nodded. "I know. Can you tow it to the nearest tire shop?"

"Not your lucky day," the man behind the counter noted as he filled out the work order.

I nodded in agreement. One of the grease monkeys came in from the shop and marched behind the counter. "That your Explorer with the two flats?" he asked.

"Yes," I replied.

"We can't repair either one—sidewalls are shot."

I frowned. "Can you match the two good ones?" I asked.

"Which ones would that be?"

I looked at him curiously. "The ones that aren't flat. You know, the back ones," I said.

"Oh, those. Well, we can't match them exactly. They aren't what I'd call good, though. You probably only have a couple thousand left on them, and your spare is balder than my Uncle Artie, and believe me, he's as hairless as they come."

My shoulders drooped in despair. I was going to have to dip into my paint-job money to buy new tires. "Okay. Let's put four new tires all around. Can we use one of the not-so-good rear tires to replace the spare?" I asked.

"You bet," he assured me.

I sat in one of the hard plastic chairs in the showroom

and paged through a magazine while I waited. I'd gotten halfway through an article about the rise in teenage smoking and wondered how anyone with half a brain could start smoking in this day and age, with all the evidence of the cancer risks and emphysema. These kids won't think smoking is so cool when every breath they take is a struggle and their best friend is an oxygen tank. The tire mechanic interrupted my reading.

"We found something weird with your spare," he announced.

"Weird?"

"Yeah. Wanna come see?" he said, gesturing me toward the door.

I followed him out to the shop, past the sign that warned against customers entering the work area. My Explorer was hoisted up in the air. He led me to a device used to remove the tires from the rims. The rim bolted to the apparatus was wrapped in duct tape, with a strange bulge on one side.

"What's that?" I asked.

"Don't know. Thought maybe you'd know, since it's your car."

"I just bought it today. I haven't a clue."

"Well, we can cut the tape off and see what it is," he offered.

I nodded. "Let's do that."

He pulled a pocketknife from his jeans and started slicing the heavy gray tape. When he finished removing the tape, he handed me the item that had been stuck to the inside rim of the spare tire. It was a woman's small leather purse. "Yours?" he asked, as he handed it to me.

"I guess it is now," I replied, taking it from him. I wandered back into the waiting room and sat down with my new "extra" while he finished putting the tires on.

It was a stylish brown leather purse fashioned like a small backpack. I lifted the outer flap and loosened the drawstring that held it closed. I pulled the items out one by one and laid them on the table in front of me: a pair of sunglasses in a hard plastic case, a small hairbrush, a lipstick, two compacts for blusher and pressed powder, an address book, an unopened book of thirty-three-cent stamps, an envelope, and a wallet. I checked all the pockets for anything else. I found a pack of cinnamon gum and a roll of breath mints. I regarded the stamps for a moment. Stamps hadn't been thirty-three cents for almost a year.

I was about to open the wallet when the tire mechanic pushed through the doors. "All set," he announced, handing me the keys.

"You're done?" I asked, surprised at how quickly he finished.

"Yep. You're ready to roll."

I quickly stuffed all the items back in the purse.

"Find anything exciting?" he asked.

"No. Just the usual stuff," I replied, pulling the drawstring tight.

"Pretty weird, hiding a purse inside a tire, don't you think?" he said.

I nodded in agreement. "Yeah. It's weird, all right."


I parked the Explorer in my usual spot at the marina. My neighbor, Mr. Cartwright, watched me walk down the dock.

"Good afternoon, Miss Lace," he greeted, in his usual formal manner.

"Hi, Mr. Cartwright," I replied.

"Is that your new vehicle?" he asked, motioning toward the Explorer sitting in the parking lot.

My eyes followed the direction of his pointing finger. "Yes, it is. I bought it today."

"It's orange," he noted.

I smiled as I stepped over the railing. "Is it?"


I grabbed a bottle of water from the refrigerator and sat down on the sofa with the purse. I opened it and pulled the wallet out. There was no cash and no credit cards. There were senior photos of two boys, both good-looking young men. The driver's license belonged to Diane Parker, forty-one years old, five-feet-seven inches tall, one hundred twenty-five pounds, brown hair, blue eyes. The address on the license was for an apartment in San Diego. I removed the address book and checked the front cover for a phone number. The address and phone number had been crossed out and new ones penciled in below it. The new address matched the one on Diane Parker's license. I picked up my phone and punched in the number. After one ring, a recording announced that the number was disconnected.

I stared at the purse sitting on my sofa. I figured the lowlife drug dealer stole this purse from poor Diane Parker, took the cash and credit cards for his own use, then got himself arrested and thrown in the slammer. Why he hid the purse in his spare tire was a mystery, but I gave up trying to make sense out of the actions of criminals a long time ago. I just wanted to contact Diane Parker and give her purse back.

I paged through the address book looking for other Parker names. I found two: Brad Parker, Junior and Malcom

Parker. Both addresses had a UCLA notation penciled next to them. I wondered if these were Diane's sons, and the boys in the senior pictures in her wallet. I tried both numbers, but got a recording each time. I didn't leave a message.

I thought about starting at the beginning of her address book and phoning until I found someone home who could tell me how to reach her. I glanced over at the purse sitting next to me and saw the corner of the envelope poking out the top. Maybe there was something in there that would help. It wasn't sealed, so I thought it would be okay to read it. I pulled it out, opened the sheet of paper folded up inside, and began reading:

Dear Bradley:

I'm writing you this letter because I fear you won't let me say all the things I need to say in person. I also fear your reaction. After our discussion this morning, it's clear to me that I'm making the right decision in divorcing you. I turned the other way when I knew you were unfaithful to me. I told myself it was just a phase you were going through—a phase that started after Malcom was born and lasted eighteen years. In case you wondered, I've never cheated on you. You almost convinced me of my worthlessness during our marriage. I resigned myself to the fact that the life I had was the life I'd been dealt and there was nothing I could do about it. But as the boys got older and closer to leaving the nest, I decided I needed to rethink that belief. I knew I'd never last in that house with you, without the boys there to provide some reason for living. Death looked better than any life with a man as coldhearted as you. When I began taking that thought seriously, I knew it was time to get out, for my own survival. I don't want any part of your business, or what's left of it. Whatever financial problems you're having, I'm sure you'll find a way out of them, like you always do. I'll have the house appraised, and you can either pay me half, or we can sell it and split the money. I'm keeping the Toyota, and I'll make the payments, since I'm working now. You know, I stopped loving you a long time ago, but the funny thing is, the reason I stopped loving you was because you made me feel like such a nothing. I didn't think you'd want to be loved by anyone as worthless as me. I actually stopped loving you because I thought that would make you happy. Is that insane?

Sincerely,
Diane

P.S. By the way, I like my coffee black, no cream, no sugar.


"Wow," I whispered to myself as I folded the letter and slid it back into the envelope.

I flipped the address book to the As and stuck my finger on the first entry—Melissa Anderson. I punched in the number and waited for an answer. A man's voice said, "Hello."

"Hello. Is Melissa there?" I asked.

"Yeah. Hang on."

A few seconds later, Melissa came on the line. "Hello," she said.

"Hi, Melissa. My name is Devonie Lace. I'm trying to

locate Diane Parker. I found her purse and your name and number was listed in her address book. Do you know how I can reach her?"

There was silence on the other end of the line. "Melissa? Are you there?"

"I'm here. What did you say your name was?"

"Devonie Lace. Do you know Diane?" I asked.

"Yes, I do . . . or I did. You see, she died over a year ago."

I dropped the address book in my hand. "Died! Oh, I'm so sorry, I didn't know. I just found her purse and wanted to return it."

I could hear Melissa whispering to someone next to her, "This woman found Diane's purse."

"Is there some family or someone I can contact to return the purse to? It looks like she might have had some children," I continued.

"She had two sons. They're both at UCLA. And there's Bradley, but I don't know if I'd call him."

"Bradley? Is that her husband?" I asked, knowing the answer.

"Yes, but maybe you should take the purse to the police, considering the situation," Melissa suggested.

"Police? I don't understand. Why the—"

"I have the name of the detective in charge of the investigation here, somewhere. Let me see if I can find . . . here it is—Detective Wright. You should call him and tell him about the purse," Melissa said.

"Wright?" I asked.

"Yes. Sam Wright. Here's the number," she continued.

I took out a pen and wrote down the name and number. "Can I ask how Diane died?"

Melissa was silent for a moment. Her voice sounded choked when she finally started to speak. I got the feeling she had been close to Diane Parker. "She fell. She was out running near Point Loma—Sunset Cliffs. She fell, or was . . . I don't know . . . maybe she fell off the cliff, but I think there's more to it than that. Just call Detective Wright, please."

"I will. I promise. Thank you for talking to me."

As I hung up the phone, Jason's words reverberated in my head. This was the skeleton he warned me about. I hate it when he's right.

## Chapter Three

I punched in the phone number for Detective Wright and waited for his answer.

"This is Wright," he announced into the phone.

"Hello. My name is Devonie Lace. Melissa Anderson gave me your number. I found Diane Parker's purse and she suggested I call you," I explained.

It sounded like he dropped the phone. I waited for the commotion to stop, then he came back on the line. "Excuse me. Spell your name," he requested, and I complied.

"Where did you find the purse?" he asked.

I explained the details and read him the letter, and I could tell he was taking notes.

"Did you ever find who killed her?" I asked.

"Diane Parker's death was an accident. Those cliffs are unstable. Signs are posted; she just ignored them," he said.

"But now that you have this letter, doesn't it sound like her husband might be a suspect?" I asked.

"I don't see how. Anyway, it's a police matter. I'd like

to come pick up the purse and take a look at your vehicle. What's your address?"

I checked my watch. I had a dinner date with Craig, and I didn't want to be late. "I have an appointment tonight, but can I bring it to you tomorrow morning? It would be more convenient for me," I explained.

"You'll bring your vehicle?" he asked.

"Yes. You won't want to keep it, will you?" I asked, biting my lip and worrying about being immobile again.

"I doubt it. Just want to get some numbers off it."

"Okay. I'll bring it by the station in the morning," I promised, then hung up the phone.

I gathered up Diane Parker's purse and jogged up the dock to the parking area. I slid the key into the Explorer's ignition and gave it a turn. It started without hesitation, but when I tried to put it in reverse, there was a terrible grinding sound. I double-clutched it and tried again until I found my gear. I chalked it up to being out of practice with a manual transmission.

I rang the bell and waited on Craig's porch until he opened the door. He shot me a panicked look. "You have to go away. I'm expecting my fiancée any minute," he said, peering around me as if he were looking for another person.

I grinned at him.

"Oh, wait. You *are* my fiancée." He gave me a huge smile and a hug. "Why do you ring the bell? I gave you a key. This is your house, too."

Standing there with his arms wrapped around me made me feel safer and happier than I'd ever been. My whole life, I'd fought those feelings, sure that once I allowed my-self some happiness, someone would take it away from me.

"This is your house. It won't be our house until we're married, and even then, I'm not sure it'll feel like it's mine."

Craig wasn't listening to me. His gaze went past me to the Explorer parked in the driveway. "What's that?" he asked.

I turned to see what had his attention. "Oh, that's my new ride. Like it?"

He gawked for a few more seconds. "Explorer?"

"Yeah," I answered as I walked past him through the doorway. He continued to study the vehicle in his driveway.

"Those are good," he noted, with a little hesitation.

"That's what I hear. Did you notice it's orange?" I asked.

"Almost right away." He squinted harder at it. "What's that green writing on the side?"

I pulled Diane Parker's letter to her estranged husband out of the purse and handed it to him. "Sunkist. Here, read this. It'll break your heart."

"Sunkist?" he asked, staring at the letter, confused.

I kissed him. "That's what I love about you. You didn't feel the need to inform me of the color of my new car. You're so considerate."

He kissed me back. "No. You're a bright girl. I just figured you probably already knew it was orange. What's this letter?"

I started down the hallway to his office. "Read it, then I'll fill you in on how I found it. Can I use your copy machine?"

"Sure. Might have to put some paper in it."

I copied all the pages from Diane's address book. Craig wandered in with the letter and handed it to me. I placed it facedown on the glass and pressed the COPY button.

"So the purse was in the spare tire?" Craig marveled.

"Weird, huh?"

Craig nodded. "Why are you making copies?"

"Because I have to give the originals to Detective Wright. He doesn't think Bradley Parker's a suspect. He thinks Diane Parker fell off that cliff all by herself. I bet he won't even go talk to Parker."

Craig frowned. "You're not going to jump in the middle of this, are you?"

"No. I just—Didn't that letter tear you up? Someone has to be on her side." I folded the letter and slid it back into the envelope. "I think Bradley Parker pushed her," I said.

"I have to admit, the guy sounds like a total sleazebag, but how can you be sure? What about the guy who hid the purse in the tire? Don't you think he's a more likely suspect?"

I stuffed the envelope back into the purse. "I hadn't thought of that. You could have something there. See? That's why I need your help with this. You're brilliant."

Craig shook his head. "If I were brilliant, I'd come up with a way to talk you out of this."

"Can't be done," I reminded him.

"I know. That's why I'm going to help you."

I kissed him again. "That's the other reason I love you."

"Because I let you wrap me around your little finger?" he joked.

"No. Because you never try to change me."


The sergeant behind the desk announced my arrival to Detective Wright over the phone. I waited several minutes before the six-foot-four, three-hundred-pound powerhouse of a man strode into the lobby. I stood in the middle of the room with Diane's purse clutched to my chest.

"Miss Lace?" he inquired, holding out his hand.

I felt dwarfed by this man. I released my grip on the purse and held my hand out. "Yes," I replied.

I shook his hand. It was warm and dry and strong.

"Is that the purse?" he asked.

I nodded and handed it to him. "This is it. Everything's still inside."

He took the purse and gave it a brief inspection. He didn't open it. "Let's get a look at the vehicle. Is it outside?"

I nodded again. "It's in the lot." He followed me out the door and down the steps. I stopped in front of the Explorer.

"This it?" he asked.

"Yes."

He removed a stubby pencil and a small notebook from his pocket and flipped through the pages. "You bought it yesterday?" he asked.

"Yes. At the U.S. Marshal's auction." I hesitated a moment while he jotted something down. "Do you want to see the letter?" I asked.

He either didn't hear me, or ignored my question. He set the purse on the hood, moved to the windshield, and cupped his hand over an area in the lower driver's side to shade the sunlight. He repeated the letters and numbers of the vehicle identification number as he wrote them down in his notebook.

"The letter's in the purse, in case you're interested," I reminded him.

He squinted at me. "I assume it's in the purse. You haven't removed anything, have you?"

"No. I just didn't want you to forget about—"

"I won't forget," he interrupted. "Did you find anything else unusual in the vehicle?"

"No. Just the purse," I answered.

"Not surprised. They usually take these things apart and put them back together before they auction them off. Guess no one ever thought to check inside the tires."

I stared at the purse on the hood. "You think the drug dealer who owned this before I bought it killed Diane Parker?"

Detective Wright rolled his eyes and shook his head. "I told you before, her death was an accident. She was jogging on the trails around Point Loma and got too close to the edge. Happens once in a while."

I folded my arms across my chest. "Then why would her purse wind up stashed inside the spare tire of a convicted drug dealer? Sounds suspicious to me."

The big man snatched the purse off the hood. "Look. This is none of your concern. It's a police matter. We've investigated the death of Diane Parker and concluded it was an accident."

He walked away and headed toward the doors of the station. I followed. "But now that you have new evidence, don't you think you should reopen the investigation?"

He stopped and glared at me. "I'll look at the contents of the purse and if I find anything suspicious, I'll follow up on it. Okay with you?" he snapped.

I sensed that I irritated this man like a gnat fluttering around his face. I didn't care. For some reason, I felt a kinship with Diane Parker, and I wanted justice for her. I looked him square in the eye. "I don't think so. You don't seem sincere, Detective Wright."

A crevice formed in his brow between the deep-set brown eyes. He stared down his chiseled nose at me, towering over my small frame. I could see the muscles of his powerful jaws clench as he formulated his next sentence. "I've never been more sincere in my entire life. If Diane Parker was murdered, I'll find out who did it. Do not get in my way. Do not tell me how to do my job. And do not suppose that you are more qualified to get to the truth than I am. Understand?"

My neck felt the strain in its awkward position as my own muscles tensed. I returned his glare. "Would it be possible for me to see what you've come up with so far in your investigation?" I asked.

He stared at me for a moment, then turned his gaze to the sky. He let out a loud, boisterous laugh. "That's priceless!" he boomed.

I remained serious. "What's so funny?" I asked.

He flashed his straight white teeth at me in a grin so broad I could almost count his fillings. "You don't see the humor? I think it's funnier than heck. Some little . . . I don't know, whatever you are . . . comes bouncing in off the street and you think you can do a better job than the entire San Diego police department. It's hilarious."

I felt my fingernails dig into the palms of my hands as my fists clenched. "So can I see your report on Diane's death?" I pressed.

"No," he barked, then walked off.

I started after him. "But—"

"No, Miss Lace," he repeated.

"I just want to—"

"No! N-O! *No!* Are you deaf?"

I stopped and watched him disappear through the doors

into the police station. My face felt hot and flushed. "What a jerk," I grumbled as I climbed into the cab of the Explorer.

I checked my watch. I was supposed to meet Craig for lunch before our appointment with a local photographer. My heart was racing, and I needed to calm down. I decided to drive to Pacific Beach. No matter how long I live here, I never lose the thrill I feel when I drive over the last rise between the ocean and me, and the glorious view of the sparkling blue Pacific paints itself across my windshield.

I hunted for a parking spot for twenty minutes. I finally found one a mile away, hiked down to the beach, removed my shoes, and rolled up the cuffs of my jeans. I walked along the shore and watched the activities going on. A group of teenagers played volleyball, laughing, concerned with nothing more than keeping the ball in the air. A pair of tan young men flung a Frisbee back and forth, challenging each other to jump a little higher with each toss. A little girl built a sand castle with a bright-pink bucket. Her father helped her by digging a moat to divert the water and keep it from washing her hard work away.

I let the water splash up around my ankles and felt its coolness work its way up my body. In a matter of minutes, I'd sent the memory of my confrontation with Detective Wright out to sea. He wasn't worth getting upset over.

I met Craig at a little sidewalk café near Old Town. He spotted me across the crowd and waved to get my attention. I made my way through the tables and stopped under the umbrella of the table he'd picked for us. I slung my purse across the back of the chair opposite his. He stood up and gave me a kiss. "Hi there," he said, squeezing my hand.

I smiled. "Hi."

We both sat down. He watched me closely. "What's wrong?" he asked.

"Nothing," I answered.

He smiled. "Uh-uh. What's wrong?" he repeated.

He wasn't going to accept my non-answer. I don't know exactly when or where it happened, but he had somehow gotten to know me better than I even know myself. Maybe it was during those months sailing around the Caribbean, taking care of me and making sure I was safe. There's no way I could ever deceive him. I took a deep breath. "I took the purse to Detective Wright this morning."

Craig watched my face, waiting for me to continue. "And . . . ?"

I fidgeted with a pack of sugar in a container on the table. "I don't think I brought out the best in him."

## Chapter Four

Spencer answered his direct line on the third ring. I was surprised, because calls usually rolled over to his voice mail. "Spencer. It's Devonie," I announced.

"Devonie! I got the wedding invitation. I thought you were never getting married. Isn't that what you told me?"

I spoke seriously. "I decided it might not be a bad idea to have a man around, you know, to open jars and stuff."

Spencer laughed. "Who is he? Do I know him?"

"He's a great guy. I met him last year when I got mixed up with that storage unit caper."

Spencer whistled into the phone. "When those guys blew up your boat?" he asked.

"That's the one." I sat at the galley table of the *Plan C* and doodled on a tablet of paper sitting in front of me. Spencer still worked for the State of California. He'd been offered a prestigious position with Bates Corporation, but was forced to turn it down. He had made an agreement with the Department of Justice to work *for* them rather than against them after being caught hacking into some presumably secure computer sites. When he tried to give notice to his boss, he was reminded of his indentured status as a State employee. He gave up his dream of driving a Pantera company car and resigned to the fact that he'd be paying for his lapse of good judgment for a few more years. At the time, I was sorry the Bates opportunity didn't materialize, but now, I was glad for it. His position with the State gives him access to a huge volume of information that would otherwise be inaccessible to me. I felt a twinge of guilt for that thought.

I'd spent a long time thinking about Wright's assessment that Bradley Parker wasn't guilty of killing his wife. I'd also thought about Craig's comment that the drug dealer who'd hidden the purse looked guiltier than the husband. I questioned my own intuition and thought it couldn't hurt to pursue the possibility that my first assumption could be wrong.

"Spencer. Can you do me a favor?" I asked.

"I knew it," he complained.

"What?"

"You never call just to shoot the breeze. You always want something. I'm nothing but a channel of information for you. You use me like a pawn in a chess game. You take advantage of my good nature. I don't know why I continue to be your friend."

I tapped my pencil on the table. "Are you finished?" I asked.

"Yes," he replied.

"Good. Here's what I need."

\*    \*    \*

Spencer tracked down the name and current address of the previous owner of my Explorer: William Mendenhal— R. J. Donovan Correctional Facility at Rock Mountain. Spencer helped cut through the red tape so I could get a visitation date to see Mr. Mendenhal. I had questions that only he could answer.

I sat opposite Willy Mendenhal. There was a short wooden barrier placed vertically on the table between us. He had no idea who I was or why I was visiting him. He was not an attractive man. His eyes were small and beady and set too close together. His hairline landed somewhere in the center of the top of his skull. The thin, dry, frizzy hair he had left was brown and tied in a ponytail at the back of his head. He was gaunt and his cheekbones stood out like shelves on the sides of his face. His teeth were crooked and yellow from neglect. It hurt my eyes to look at him.

He leered at me. "You one of those gals lookin' for a prison pen pal?"

"No," I replied.

"Too bad." He pointed to an inmate across the room who was visiting with another woman. "Guy over there just got engaged to his pen pal. Never even met her till she decided she wanted to save some poor soul from the grips of the devil."

The thought of a relationship with the creature seated in front of me turned my stomach. If he had a soul to save, I wasn't going to be the one to take on the challenge. "I bought your Ford Explorer at an auction."

He stared at me with a blank expression.

"The orange one," I continued.

"So?" he replied. "You want your money back? Talk to the jerks who put me in this place."

I leaned forward on my elbows and spoke quietly. "I had a little tire trouble—the spare," I said.

His stare intensified. "Yeah? What kind of trouble?" he asked.

"I found the purse," I told him.

His beady eyes shifted around the room. "I don't know nothin' about no purse."

I expected this response. I was prepared. "Funny. My friend who works for the DOJ found your fingerprints all over it and the duct tape holding it to the rim," I bluffed.

He looked like he wanted to cry. He leaned in closer to me and whispered as desperately as he could. "I didn't have nothin' to do with that lady they found. I swear it."

"Then why'd you hide her purse in the tire?" I asked.

He didn't answer.

I pressed a little. "I think you pushed her over the edge. I bet the police would agree."

He shook his head. "No way. I found the purse and used her credit card before I saw on the news that she was dead. I knew if they traced her card to me, I'd be lookin' down worse charges than stealin' and dealin'."

Getting information out of this guy was easier than I thought it would be. Only problem was, he could be lying through his teeth.

"I still don't see why you hid the purse," I said.

He wiped the orange sleeve of his prison overalls on his forehead. "Bennie told me Jocko snitched on me. The narcs were on their way to my place. Bennie has a tire shop downtown. He helped me stash the purse. I read that letter—you seen it?"

I nodded.

He continued. "Looked to me like the lady's old man probably offed her. I figured I didn't want to lose track of the purse, in case someone tried to pin the lady's fall on me. I'd get that letter and show 'em who they ought to be lookin' for."

"So you never told anyone about the purse?" I asked.

"Why would I? No one ever said anything about the lady."

I tapped my fingers on the table. I thought he could be telling the truth. "How'd you get the purse in the first place?" I asked.

His eyes shifted around the room, again. "Lady's car sat out there for a couple of days. I figured it was deserted. Had a decent stereo, and a bunch of CDs sittin' on the seat. I busted the window to snatch the stuff. Just thought I'd check the trunk. The purse was in there. Had some cash—and the credit cards I told you about. Easy pickins," he bragged.

I thanked Willy for the information and pushed my chair out from the table.

He winked and flashed his slimy-toothed grin at me. "Sure you don't wanna be pen pals? Gets awful lonesome in here, if you know what I mean."

I forced a pained smile. "No, thanks."

As I headed for the exit, he called across the room. "Then can we just get married? I think I might love you."

I waited impatiently to be let through the exit doors before Willy launched any more proposals across the room. I felt a powerful urge to stop at the store and buy a bottle of antibacterial soap.

*   *   *

I'd never seen anyone's face turn the shade of red that Sam Wright's did as I sat across from him at his desk.

"You did what?" he hissed.

"I went to see Willy Mendenhal. He's the previous registered owner of my Explorer," I replied.

"I know who he is." Wright glared at me. The veins in his neck popped out and I could see his jaw clenching again. "I want to know why you would do such a stupid thing."

"It wasn't stupid," I defended. "In fact, he was very helpful."

The pencil Wright held in his clenched fist broke in two. "And furthermore, how did you even know how to find the guy? That's not the kind of stuff you get from the phone book."

I felt the pace of my heart speed up a little. I couldn't tell him how I got the information, or Spencer would be in big trouble. "That's not important. Last I checked, it's still a free country, and I can go visit whoever I want—prisoner or not." I moved to the edge of my seat and glared back at Wright. "What is important is that you have not gone to see Willy Mendenhal. You've done absolutely nothing with the evidence I've given you. A woman is dead, and you're sitting here on your big . . . muscles, doing nothing!"

Wright picked up the two halves of the broken pencil from his desk and broke them again. I had the feeling he'd get some satisfaction doing the same thing to my neck. He took a deep breath. "As it so happens, I was on my way to see Mr. Mendenhal when you showed up and dropped your little bomb in my lap."

I sat back in my chair. "Good. Then you'll probably want to talk to me after, so we can compare stories."

Wright dropped the broken pieces of yellow pencil on his desktop and cradled his forehead in his hands. "Tell me what he told you," he moaned.

"Right now? I thought—"

"Yes. Right now, before I wring your little neck and you won't be able to talk at all," he snapped.

"Why are you so hostile? I'm only trying to help."

Wright pushed the broken pencil pieces off the edge of his desk into a trash can. He opened his desk drawer and pulled out a fresh new pencil and proceeded to sharpen it. "Before I joined the force, I was a building contractor up in L.A. County. I used to give people two versions of every bid. One price to do the job—another price, doubled, to do the same job if the customer wanted to help."

I studied his face. The red flush crept up from his shirt collar. "You need to relax, Detective Wright. Take it from someone who knows. You're on your way to a massive coronary."

He reached into his desk drawer again and pulled out a bottle of aspirin. He popped two in his mouth and washed them down with a swallow of soda from an aluminum can. "Just tell me about your conversation with Willy Mendenhal."

"Well, first of all, he didn't kill Diane Parker," I said.

"You're kidding. He told you that?" Wright interrupted, not hiding the sarcasm in his voice.

"Can I finish?" I asked.

"Go ahead," he allowed.

"He also thinks Bradley Parker pushed Diane off the cliff."

"Well, there you go. Mystery solved. Let's all go home.

The drug dealer answered all our questions and did our job for us."

I glared at the arrogant man across from me, rocking back in his swivel chair. I'd have given a hundred dollars to see that chair go all the way over, knocking the wind out of his sails. "It's a wonder you can solve any crimes at all, considering how narrow-minded you are," I said.

He forced a smile. "I have half a mind to arrest you for interfering with a criminal investigation. You won't like spending the night in the lockup."

"According to you, there was no crime, so how can there be an investigation for me to interfere with?"

Snap. The new pencil was now two short stubs. "I've reopened the investigation. Stay out of my way. Let me do my job. Do not help. Is that clear?"

"Perfectly," I replied.

"Good. Now tell me what Mendenhal said."

I stared at Wright for a long moment, but didn't say anything. I glanced down at my jeans and noticed a loose thread. I tugged at it to break it free.

"What are you doing?" Wright demanded.

"Not helping. Isn't that what you want?"

"For crying out loud! You are the most exasperating woman I've ever come across. Do you irritate everyone this way, or am I just lucky?"

I smiled at Detective Sam Wright. He would be a challenge, but eventually, I'd get to him—if he didn't kill me first.

## Chapter Five

I scanned through microfiche records looking for all the newspaper accounts of Diane Parker's death. Her body was found on the rocks at the base of a cliff near Point Loma. A young couple discovered her when they were climbing over the rocks, trying to get back to the trail that led up to higher ground before the tide came in. The reports didn't provide many details. She was wearing running shoes and appeared to be a jogger. It was the fall that killed her, not a stroke or a bullet. She was covered with bruises, but those could have come from the fall. She had been dead two days before being discovered. Her vandalized car was found shortly after she was. The location where her car was found was described, and a picture of it, with its broken window and open trunk, appeared in the lower corner of the page. I printed out the last article and gathered up my things.

I slid into the Explorer and slammed the door. I checked my watch. Craig was working at the hospital and wouldn't be finished with his patients until later in the evening. I didn't want to do what I was considering doing by myself. I slid the key into the ignition and started the engine. I cringed when I heard a loud grinding as I shoved the gearshift into reverse. I resolved to practice my clutching skills before I did some real damage.

I parked in front of Jason's Appliance and Repair Shop. Jason was busy attaching the canvas strapping around a large side-by-side refrigerator so he could dolly it into the shop. He saw me approach and smiled. "Hey, Dev. Give me a hand?"

I stopped and grinned. I couldn't resist. I began applauding.

"Very funny. I mean help me. Rocky went out for doughnuts, and this thing's too big for me to handle by myself," Jason complained.

I stepped up to the big appliance. "Okay. What do you want me to do?"

"Just get on the other side and push the top over when I tell you to," he instructed.

"Okay," I said, placing my hands against the refrigerator.

Ever since leaving the library, I wondered how I would convince Jason to help me. He'd never go along if he knew what I was up to. As we maneuvered the big refrigerator through the doors, I started my pitch. "Can you get away from the shop for a little while?" I asked.

"What for?"

"I need you to help me with something," I replied.

We rolled the dolly around a corner and Jason stopped. "This is good, right here. Let's let her down," he instructed. "Help you with what?" he asked, as he untied the straps around the appliance.

"I want to go check out something at Point Loma. You know that area pretty well, don't you?"

Jason eyed me suspiciously. "Yeah. What is it you want to check out?"

"Just something I saw in the paper. I know there are cliffs and rocks out there. I'm not sure about the tides. I don't want to get stranded or fall off a cliff or anything," I explained.

"What about your hero, Craig? Can't he help you?"

"He's busy at the hospital, saving lives. You're just here, fixing refrigerators." I winked at him, knowing he wouldn't be offended by my remark. We've been friends too long.

"Uh-huh." He squinted at me. "I can't leave the shop till Rocky gets back."

I nodded. "Right. With the doughnuts. Thought you were gonna give those up."

"No. I said I'd cut back on the doughnuts. I never said I'd give them up."

I shrugged my shoulders. "Whatever. So you'll come with me?"

Jason folded his arms across his chest. "Will I regret it?" he asked.

"Will you regret seeing my body being fished out of the surf because I fell off a cliff or got caught in the tide?" I retorted.

Jason screwed his face up into a painful-looking contortion. "I hate it when you do this."

"Do what?" I asked, innocently.

"You know what. I know you're up to something, otherwise you'd come out and tell me what's out at Point Loma," he complained.

"I'll tell you the whole story on the way. Hey, you want to drive? You haven't seen my new Ford yet," I baited.

"Yeah? You picked it up at that auction?" he asked.

"Yep. Explorer. Got a good deal."

The bell on the front door rang, and Rocky came strolling into the shop with a pink bakery box. I followed Jason out to the showroom floor.

"Watch the shop for me, Rocky. I've gotta help Dev with something," Jason said.

Rocky stuffed half of a glazed doughnut in his mouth. He nodded, unable to speak. His mouth was so full, he could barely close his lips. Jason peeked in the pink box and grabbed a maple bar. He motioned to me. "Help yourself," he offered.

I smirked at him. "No, thanks. Wouldn't want to deprive you of your sugar fix."


I handed Jason the keys as we stood next to the Explorer. He gawked at the writing on the door, then laughed: "The Sunkist-mobile. You bought this?"

I walked around to the passenger side door. "It was a great deal. You want to drive or not?"

Jason started the engine and depressed the clutch. The awful grinding sound pierced the air as he put it into reverse. "Whoa. I think you better have the transmission checked out," he said.

I nodded. "I thought it was just me. I'll take it into the shop when I get a chance."

I waited until we were nearly to Point Loma before I pulled the printouts of the newspaper articles out of my purse. I read the description of the location where Diane

Parker's car was found to Jason. "You know where that is?" I asked.

"Yeah. That's where we're headed?"

"Yes," I replied.

Jason pulled over to the side of the road and parked. I gaped at him. "Why are we stopping?" I asked.

Jason pointed his finger in my face. His eyebrows nearly met in the deep furrow between them. I'd seen that look on his face before. He was angry. "We aren't moving another inch until you tell me the whole story," he announced.

"I told you. I just want to go look around."

Jason opened the driver's side door and stepped out. He started walking back the direction we'd come from.

"Where are you going?" I demanded. I piled out of the passenger side door and chased after him. He kept moving.

"Back to the shop. Find someone else's life to mess up today. I'm not interested in another Devonie fiasco."

I stopped and watched him march down the street. I wracked my brain for some way to stop him. I called out to him. "If I tell you the whole story, will you come with me?"

He didn't miss a step. He kept walking.

"Jason! Please. I'll tell you everything, but I'm scared. I don't want to go out there alone," I pleaded.

He stopped and turned. "You tell me the story, then I'll tell you whether I'll go or not."

I told him about the purse in the spare tire, the letter Diane Parker wrote to her husband, the visit out to the Donovan State Prison, the confrontation with Sam Wright, and I showed him the copies of the newspaper articles I'd gotten from the library. He studied the papers and shook his head. "I can't believe you, Dev. Why don't you listen to that detective and stay out of this?"

"Because I think someone killed Diane Parker. I think maybe her husband killed her, but mostly, I want to find out the truth."

Jason took my shoulders in his hands and gave me a gentle shake. "The police will get to the truth. They don't need you to get in the middle of it. You could get hurt."

I shook his hands off my shoulders and took a step back. "She's been dead for over a year. The police aren't looking. Someone owes Diane Parker's sons the truth. Someone owes Diane Parker her life. Someone has to find justice in this."

"But it doesn't have to be you, Dev," he offered.

I turned and started back toward the Explorer. "Then who? I'm going out there to look around. You can come, or you can stay. I'm scared, but I'm not a coward. I won't let my fear stop me."

I climbed up into the driver's seat and slammed the door shut. I checked the rearview mirror. Jason walked toward me, waving. "Wait! I'll go with you. I'm a fool, and I know I'll regret it before it's over, but I won't be able to live with myself if anything happens to you."

We parked in the same area where Diane's car had been found. The place was deserted. The only evidence that anything ever happened there was a few scattered pieces of broken window glass. I scanned through the newspaper articles again. According to the last story, Diane's body was found about a mile from where her car was parked. I surveyed the area, looking for a trail, but couldn't see any obvious signs of one.

"You hike out here, don't you?" I asked Jason.

"Yeah. Trail's over this way," he said, as he started off toward a stand of trees.

I followed him. When he got to the trail, he headed north. "How do we know which direction she went?" I asked.

"We don't, but I know the landscape a mile this direction, and there's a few good spots to get yourself killed if you get too close to the edge," he answered.

We'd been walking for over thirty minutes and had seen a few places that could have been the site of Diane's fall. There was no detailed description of the exact place in any of the newspaper stories and I knew I'd never get Detective Sam "Always" Wright to cut loose with any information. Jason walked about ten yards ahead of me, whistling as he enjoyed the scenery. I spotted something yellow hanging from the branch of a tree near the trail and stopped. "Hold up, Jason," I called.

It must have been a remnant of the yellow crime-scene tape the police string up around areas that are under investigation. This section of trail was about twenty yards from the cliffs. We walked over to the edge and peered over. The foamy surf gurgled around the jagged rocks protruding from the ocean floor. I felt a little dizzy looking down and took a step back.

"Her body must have been found on those rocks," I concluded. "I wonder if she fell here, or if her body was washed up on the rocks with the high tide?"

Jason glanced up and down the coast and studied the rocks below. "She fell from here," he stated, as if he'd seen the whole thing happen.

"How can you tell?" I asked.

"Because it's high tide right now. The rocks are well out of the water. For her to have been on those rocks, she would have had to come from above, because the ocean wasn't going to wash her up on them," he explained.

I backed away from the edge and turned toward the trail. "I just want to look around, see if there's anything weird here."

Jason followed me. "You're not gonna find anything. That yellow tape means the police already went over it with a fine-toothed comb," he said.

I crossed the trail and scanned the ground on the east side of it. "Maybe. If that yellow tape was the corner marker of where they searched, I'll just look a little further. They could have missed something," I said hopefully.

Jason took up the search a few yards north of my position. We wove back and forth, kicking the leaves and dirt around whenever anything out of the ordinary caught our attention. We managed to turn up a few empty beer bottles, a couple of candy wrappers, and a knotted mess of fishing line. I checked my watch. We'd been searching for nearly an hour. I finally concluded that Jason was right. We weren't going to find anything. If there was something to be found, Detective Wright most likely had it in his possession, and I'd never know anything about it.

"You were right," I admitted. "I guess we may as well go home." I started back toward the trail.

Jason caught my arm and turned me the other direction. "The trail makes a turn back there. Remember?" he said, pointing. "If we cut through these trees, we'll get to the car sooner."

My eyes followed the direction of his outstretched arm. "Are you sure?" I questioned.

"Yes," he stated.

"But—"

"Are you going to argue with me? The girl who can't find her way out of San Diego unless she keeps the ocean on her left shoulder?"

I didn't say a word. I just fell in step behind Jason and followed his lead. He was right. I can barely navigate my way out of a mall parking lot. I followed closely and gawked at the trees as we passed. I wasn't paying attention and didn't notice that he'd stopped.

"What's this?" he pondered, just before I plowed into the back of him. I just about knocked us both to our knees.

"Sorry! I didn't see you stop," I apologized.

Jason knelt down and inspected the black fabric protruding from the ground. I squatted down next to him. "What is it?" I asked.

The black fabric was about an inch wide and it was Velcro. He pulled on it and the remainder of the fabric came up with it. It was about a foot long and a couple of inches wide. It looked like a series of small quilted pillows, but it was heavy. "It's a weight," Jason concluded. "A wrist or ankle weight—like runners wear."

I took the black object from him. "Runners? Diane was running when she fell. I wonder if this was hers?"

Jason stood up straight. "If it was, what was it doing way over here, so far from the trail?" he wondered.

"That's a good question," I said. I crawled around on the ground and searched for the other weight. I pushed leaves and dirt around and inspected every unusual-looking twig. "What are *we* doing over here, so far from the trail?" I said.

"Taking a short cut to the car," Jason offered.

"Right. And if you were running from someone who

might want to hurt you, wouldn't you go for the shortcut, too?" I speculated.

Jason nodded. "And I'd probably try to lose those ankle weights, if I could."

I stood up and brushed the dirt and leaves off my knees. "Come on. The other one's not here. Let's get back to the car."

I dropped Jason off at his shop. Before returning home to the *Plan C*, I stopped to pick up a bottle of wine and a few things to fix the fabulous dinner I'd promised Craig later that night. He tells me he loves my cooking. Every time he takes the first bite of a meal I've prepared, he stops chewing, rolls his eyes, and acts as though he's died and gone to heaven. The moment I knew I just had to hang on to him was when he asked for seconds of my whole-wheat pizza topped with tofu cheese and turkey sausage. How many men can there be out there who would actually look forward to that? He's got to be one in a million.

As I strolled down the aisles of the grocery store, I came to the conclusion that I was going to need Detective Wright's help if there was any connection between Diane Parker and the ankle weight we'd found. That wasn't going to be easy. I wandered down the aisles until I found the row I was looking for. I gazed at the overwhelming collection of school supplies dangling from a million hooks and pegs.

## Chapter Six

I sat across from Sam Wright at his desk and gave him the biggest, brightest smile I could muster. I'd worried about this meeting all night, and as a result, didn't get much sleep. He didn't return my smile.

"What are you doing here, Miss Lace?" he asked, with a discouraging tone in his voice.

I didn't say anything. I kept smiling, opened my purse, and pulled out a brand-new box of fresh pencils. I laid them on his desk and meekly pushed them across the blotter until they were directly in front of him. He eyed them curiously, then picked them up.

"What the—?"

"It's sort of a peace offering," I said. "And apparently a tension reliever, too."

I watched his face for a reaction. For a moment, I thought the man was made of stone. If he dared smile, his face might crack. He regarded the box of pencils as though I'd just handed him a hand grenade. Finally, he took his

54

eyes off them and turned his attention to me. I raised my eyebrows in anticipation. Was he going to throw me out? Charge me with detective abuse? Have me arrested for criminal pestering? I slumped in my chair, waiting for the tongue-lashing that was sure come.

He didn't yell at me. His face broke out into the biggest grin I'd seen since I met him. I sat up and smiled back. "You're not going to yell at me?" I asked.

"Oh, you can bet I'm going to yell at you. But this is cute—real cute."

My smile faded a bit, but I remained hopeful.

His voice returned to its normal, serious tone. "Now. Tell me what you're doing here and why I'm going to be yelling at you."

I reached across the desk and opened the box of pencils. I removed one and handed it to him. "Here. You might want this."

He leaned back in his swivel chair, folded his arms across his massive chest, and frowned at me.

I swallowed hard. "I read the newspaper articles about Diane Parker's death. They said she was jogging when she fell."

Detective Wright nodded, but did not offer any words.

"I was wondering if she was wearing ankle weights when they found her body?" I continued.

His face took on a curious expression. He sat forward in his chair and leaned on his elbows. "What makes you ask a question like that?"

"Was she?" I repeated.

If he were a dog, he would have growled. I'd learned to read his mood by the clenching of his jaw. I slid back in my chair but kept eye contact.

"I'm not going to sit here and play games with you, Miss Lace," he grumbled.

"Call me Devonie," I offered, trying to ease the mounting tension.

"Devonie. I want you to tell me why you're asking the question," he insisted.

I opened my purse, then hesitated. "My real question is, was she wearing only one ankle weight?" I removed the weight from my purse and placed it in the center of his desk. "One like this?"

He picked it up and inspected it closely. "Where'd you get this?" he demanded.

I felt my heart pick up an extra beat or two. He'd be furious with me when he learned I'd been snooping around the scene where Diane's body was found. I took a deep breath and concentrated on my delivery. "I went to the place where Diane's body was found. I was just looking around, you know, to see if maybe you missed—" I stopped. This was not a wise approach, accusing him of missing something. That would be suicide for me. "To get a fresh perspective," I finally said.

He studied me through squinting eyes, as though he were trying to make some determination about what I'd just presented to him. His jaw quit flexing and he placed the weight back down on his desk.

I cleared my throat. "So, was she? Wearing one weight?" I asked again.

He hesitated for a long moment. I sensed his struggle between keeping me in the dark and realizing I wasn't going to give up. "Diane's body was found with one ankle weight, just like this one. That fact was never publicized. We do that, to allow us to filter possible leads. You'd be amazed how many crackpots out there want to confess to crimes they read about in the papers."

I nodded. "No accident, though. Right, Detective?" I thought about the statement one second after it slipped out of my mouth. I could be treading on thin ice. This man absolutely abhorred being contradicted, or worse, accused of incompetence.

"Miss Lace—"

"Devonie," I corrected.

"Devonie. First you show up with a murder victim's purse, and a fairly incredible explanation of how you acquired it. Then, you present me with an article worn by the victim at the time of her death—an article that no one but myself and the other police officers at the scene are aware of. A detective worth his salt would look at you and see a prime suspect."

I cringed. "Is that what you see?" I asked.

He shook his head. "You're too darn annoying to be guilty. If you were the murderer, you'd leave me the heck alone, not pester me to the point of wanting to wring your scrawny little neck."

He either didn't notice my injured expression, or didn't care.

"But I still have half a mind to have you arrested for interfering with a murder investigation," he continued.

My hurt feelings retreated and were immediately replaced by anger. I felt my grasp on diplomacy slip through my fingers. "Well now, that would be par for how you've managed this investigation, wouldn't it?" I said, trying desperately to maintain control. "I've brought you more evidence in two days than you've gotten in over a year, and you can't get beyond your egotistical, more superior-than-thou attitude that only a Mister Macho detective, such as yourself, has enough brain muscle to find the truth." I grabbed the new pencil from his desk, broke it in half, and slammed the pieces back on the blotter, slapping my hands hard and flat on top of them.

He jumped in his seat and raised his eyebrows in surprise at my aggressive reaction. "Settle down, Devonie. I didn't say I was going to arrest you, only that I ought to."

"Why? To teach me a lesson? To get me out of your hair so you won't feel so incompetent for not finding the ankle weight yourself? It wasn't that hard to find, *Detective*." I emphasized the word, to make my point. "Seems to me a detective 'worth his salt,' as you put it, would look at me and see a fresh resource for a stale investigation, instead of a threat to his ego." My heart raced and I felt the dampness under my arms. I took a deep breath and braced myself for the counterattack.

He stared at me with eyes that seemed a little too understanding. "Are you through?" he asked.

I took a quick emotional inventory. I'd released most of the hostility I felt toward Sam Wright. "Yes. I think so," I announced.

He removed a fresh pencil and handed it to me. "You sure? Want to break one more, just in case?" he jested. "It can be therapeutic."

I smiled and shook my head. He'd managed to ease the tension. He started to put the pencil back in the box. "Wait," I blurted, snatching the pencil from his hand. "Maybe I will take it—for later."

Jason and I had marked the area where we found the ankle weight by piling rocks, much the same way hikers mark their path when they leave the trail. I led Detective Wright to the exact spot where we found the weight. He made notes in his small notebook and asked a few questions about the condition it was in when we found it—was it covered with leaves or was it plainly visible? He intended to bring another team of crime-scene technicians to the location and go over the area with a fine-toothed comb. I felt relief and gratification that he'd finally taken me seriously. Respect was something one must earn from Sam Wright, and I would have to prove my credibility every inch of the way.

Detective Wright slid behind the wheel and slipped on a pair of reflective sunglasses. I got in the passenger seat and buckled up. As he drove us back to the station, I admired the view of the Pacific whenever I could catch a glimpse. Finally, I asked the question that had been nagging at me all morning. "Why are you so sure Bradley Parker didn't kill Diane?"

He glanced over at me, then returned his attention to the road. He didn't answer.

"Do you think Willy Mendenhal did it?" I asked.

He continued to ignore my questions. I studied his profile and his firm jaw, set like stone. For the first time, I noticed how handsome he was. His brown hair showed a little gray at the temples. He had a few laugh lines that accentuated the character in his face. His brown eyes were large and his lashes were dark and thick. His nose was perfectly chiseled, like the statues of Greek gods I'd seen pictures of. Though he didn't have one, I thought he'd look great with a mustache.

"Ever think of growing a mustache?" I asked.

He gave me a curious glance then shook his head. "Too itchy," he replied.

"What a relief. For a minute there, I thought you'd gone deaf."

He shook his head. "Look. I'm not going to discuss aspects of this investigation that don't involve you. I want you to stay out of it. When I want information from you, I'll ask," he said.

I nodded. "So, it's a one-way street?"

"Absolutely."

"But you are looking at it as a murder and not an accident. Right?" I continued.

He nodded. "Yes. I'll concede to that. Not an accident."

"Would you concede that Bradley Parker had a motive?" I asked. As expected, he didn't answer. "Or maybe she stumbled on Willy in the middle of a drug deal out there and he shoved her over the edge?"

Wright flipped on his turn signal, glanced over his shoulder, and changed lanes. I noticed his muscular forearms and biceps. I wondered how many hours a day he spent lifting weights and working out. I estimated him to be in his early to mid forties. By now, I wasn't really expecting any response from him. I just lobbed ideas into the air to see if he'd catch them. It seemed to me they were hitting him in the chest and landing on the ground.

Wright pulled into the police station lot and parked in a slot close to the building. He reached into his pocket and pulled out a card with his name and number. He scribbled something on it. "Here," he said as he handed it to me. "You are in no way to continue snooping around about Diane Parker."

I studied the card. He'd written a phone number on it.

"But things seem to miraculously land in your lap, so if that happens, I want you to call me. I've put my home number on there, in case it lands in the middle of the night."

I slipped the card into my purse. "Okay."

"But no snooping. Got it?" he reminded me.

"Absolutely."

I slid into the driver's seat of the Explorer and glanced over at the pile of newspaper accounts of Diane's death. I pulled one from the top of the stack and skimmed down the column. Garrett Henderson was the name of the man who reported her missing when she didn't show up for work on Monday morning. He was an editor at the San Diego *Union Tribune*. I watched Detective Wright disappear into the building in front of me, then I checked my watch. "I wonder if newspaper editors take lunch?" I whispered as I backed out of the parking spot and headed out of the lot.

## Chapter Seven

Garrett Henderson shook my hand and gave me a warm smile. He was tall and slender, with the lean muscles of a swimmer or a cyclist. His dark hair was cut short on the sides and a little spiky in top. He wore round, wire-rimmed glasses which actually added to the appeal of his smooth, tanned face. I placed him in my same general age category—thirty-something—but I wouldn't have been shocked to find out he was forty. His shirtsleeves were rolled up, like a man who likes to get into his work. "You say you were a friend of Diane's?" he asked.

I smiled back at him. "More of an acquaintance," I fibbed. "I've been working with a detective on the investigation into her death and I wondered if you could tell me anything?"

"You're with the police?" he questioned.

My heart beat a bit faster. If Sam Wright found out about this, I'd be picking up garbage along the Pacific Coast Highway as part of my community service punishment until my fortieth birthday. He'd probably make me wear a sand-wich board that read: *My name is Devonie Lace, and I'm a compulsive snooper.* "No. This is purely personal," I ad-mitted.

Garrett frowned. "Darn shame about Diane. She was a real trouper. We really miss her around here," he said.

I nodded in agreement. "The paper said you were the one who reported her missing?"

"That's right. She didn't show up for work on Monday morning. That wasn't like her. She'd been here over a year and never missed a day. She'd call if she was even going to be five minutes late," he explained.

I took this all in. I had very little insight into Diane's character, except for the letter to Bradley. I hoped Garrett could paint a clearer picture for me—fill in some details. "What was her job here?" I asked.

Garrett glanced around the bustling newspaper room and motioned toward a closed door. "Let's go in my office where it's quieter."

I followed him inside. He offered me a chair, which I thankfully took.

"Diane started out as a file clerk, but she was far too talented for that. I could see it right away," he said, almost proud that he'd found a diamond in the rough.

"So she advanced?" I questioned.

"Yes. Not long before she died, I'd bumped her up to a reporter position. She'd done a couple of real slick pieces. Maybe you read them?"

I shook my head. "Maybe, but I was down in the Carib-bean last year. I didn't see too many papers."

Garrett gave me a surprised glance. "Caribbean? Sounds like a nice vacation."

"Should've been, if the circumstances were different." I didn't explain any further. I was on a mission and didn't want to get sidetracked with stories from my past. "But I'd like to know more about Diane. Do you think she was working on a story and crossed the wrong people?" I asked.

"You mean did her job get her killed?"

"I guess that's the basic gist of my question. Any idea what she was working on when she died?"

Garrett snickered. "I said she was talented, but you don't start out on the big stories. You have to cut your teeth on small stuff, like school-board meetings and plans for building new malls—nothing that would even suggest murder. Believe me, Diane's death was not related to anything she was working on here."

I frowned. This seemed like a promising direction at first—fresh new reporter, inexperienced, uncovers the illicit works of a corrupt politician and ends up fish food. Garrett sensed my disappointment.

"You ask me, her husband ought be the one under the microscope," he confided.

Our eyes met, as if we'd both discovered we had the identical thought at the same moment in time. I nodded and pointed my finger his direction. "That's exactly what I've been trying to tell the police."

Garrett sat up in his chair. "Oh, believe me, it's not like they haven't already heard it before. Do you know the first reaction from people who knew both Diane and her husband, was to assume he'd killed her?"

I raised my eyebrows and moved to the edge of my chair. "Really? And they told the police this?"

"You bet they did. We all did. The guy's a waste of

skin." Garrett stared out into space and shook his head, as though he were recalling an unpleasant morbid scene.

"Did you know her husband?" I asked.

"Never met him. But she'd told me enough to know he's a lowlife, two-timing, arrogant son-of-a—a real scoundrel, if you know what I mean," Garrett explained, with the look of disgust still on his face.

I knew exactly what he meant. There's no pain greater than the realization that the person you've devoted your entire adult life to, the person you trusted with your most intimate thoughts and dreams—your entire being—has no more regard for you than a speck of dust. To be betrayed by the one person in the world you thought you could count on is almost unbearable. To realize that for so many years, you never really had what you thought you had, that the whole relationship was based on a misconception—a lie— is more than anyone should have to endure. Yes, I knew exactly what he was talking about, and my kinship with Diane Parker grew tenfold in that moment. I made a conscious decision that I'd see this to the end—I'd keep looking. I'd pester Sam Wright until he got so sick of me he'd actually take some official action against me. But I wouldn't rest until Diane's murderer was brought to justice.

I was about to leave when a thought crossed my mind. "What happened to Diane's personal belongings? The things she kept here in her desk?" I asked.

"They were all packed up and given to Bradley," he explained.

"Was there much?"

"I don't think so. I never saw it, but the clerk who packed it up said she only needed one paper box, so it couldn't have been too much. Why?" he asked.

"Just wondered," I replied.

Garrett walked me out to the parking lot. I thanked him for his time and opened the door to my Explorer, then stopped. "You know the saddest part of this whole thing?" I said.

He looked at me questioningly, waiting for me to continue.

"Even if Bradley Parker didn't kill Diane, the fact that everyone assumed he did, that he could, or even would—makes you wonder how his kids can stand to be on the same planet with him," I said.

Garrett nodded. "I don't think his kids see him as the demon everyone else sees. Oh, they know he's no saint, but think about it. Could you get out of bed every morning if you thought for an instant that your father threw your mother off a cliff? You'd convince yourself it wasn't so, for your own sanity."

With that, I slid into the driver's seat and pulled the door closed. The drive back to the marina seemed longer than it should have. I hit every red light in San Diego, or at least it felt that way.

I left a message on Spencer's voice mail to call me as soon as he could. Within ten minutes, my phone rang.

"Devonie? It's Spencer. What's up?"

"Hey, Spence. I need you to run another name for me," I requested, wasting no time.

"Sorry. No can do."

"What?"

Spencer cleared his throat and spoke quietly into the phone. "I've got a new boss and he watches me like a hawk."

I frowned. "What about from your house?" I asked.

"He's got electronic eyes. The guy raises paranoid to a whole new level. I don't think he has an ulcer, but he's definitely a carrier," Spencer joked.

"Why is he on your case?"

Spencer chuckled. "He knows about my track record. Figures once a hacker, always a hacker."

"He's right, you know," I admitted.

"Yeah. I wouldn't give his kind a second thought, but if he catches me, it's not a warning and a little slap on the wrist—it's a trip to the big house. I don't think I'd do well in jail," Spencer said.

"No. Jail wouldn't suit you. Guess I'll have to think of some other way to find out about Bradley Parker."

"What's the name again?" Spencer asked.

"Parker. Bradley Parker," I repeated.

"Why does that name sound familiar?" he said. I could hear Spencer fumbling with something on the other end of the phone.

"He owns a software consulting firm here in San Diego. Maybe you've heard of him through his company. It's called Business Solutions," I offered.

"Yeah. Here it is. I have his card. Bradley Parker. Met him last month at that big computer show over at Cal Expo. Tried to hire me. Said he was desperate for an experienced network technician."

"You met him?" I asked.

"Yeah. He found out I knew something about networks, and he latched onto me like a tick. Thought I was gonna have to douse him with kerosene."

"What was he like? Did he seem like someone who could be a killer?" I asked.

"He's a killer?" Spencer marveled.

"I don't know for sure. I do know he's a womanizing skirt chaser. What makes a man chase after women he has no intention of marrying?"

"I suppose it's the same urge that makes dogs chase cars they have no intention of driving," Spencer answered.

I laughed out loud, then remembered why I'd called. "How am I going to find out more about this guy?"

"Why don't you go to work for him? What better way to get the dirt on someone than to spend thirty percent of your time with him?"

I laughed. "You forgot about my work ethic. It's more like fifty percent."

"Only if he has the same work ethic," Spencer reminded me.

I looked up the address for Business Solutions, Inc. in the phone book. I hurried around the cabin of the *Plan C*, searching for my navy-blue pumps and a pair of pantyhose that didn't have a run or a hole in the toe. The DeskJet printer, sitting on a small table in the cabin I'd designated as an office, spit out a copy of my résumé. I buttoned my blazer and straightened the hem of my skirt. As I inspected my image in the mirror, I had a flashback to my days as a database administrator at San Tel. It must have been something similar to the experiences war veterans call shell shock. The vision of me in a navy-blue business suit, matching high heels, my hair pulled back, and makeup just right, sent me into a near-panic attack. I sat on the edge of the bed and forced my breathing to slow down. I reminded myself that this was not for real—just a tactic to get information. I was not going to rejoin the rat race; I was just going to spectate for a while.

I had to make one stop on the way to Bradley Parker's office. Ann Marie's Bridal Shop had left a message that my dress was ready, and I could pick it up any time after noon. I backed through the door carrying the gown, protected in a clear plastic bag. I draped the lacy white dress across the back of the passenger seat in an effort to keep it as wrinkle-free as possible. The simple lines and understated elegance of the dress had caught my attention the second I laid eyes on it in Ann Marie's big picture-glass window. The style looked reminiscent of the 1920s. The short cap sleeves fell just off the shoulder. It had a sheath silhouette but was slightly fitted to follow the curve of the waist and hips. The hem fell well above the ankle in front but dipped lower in the back. The layers of vanilla-colored lace made it seem as delicate as a fragile glass ornament. I remember staring at it through the window for a long time before I walked into the shop. When I saw the tiny pearl buttons stitched down the back, so many I couldn't count them, and so close they almost touched, I knew there was no other dress in the world I could possibly get married in.

I sat in the lobby of Business Solutions, Inc., résumé in hand, and waited for Bradley Parker to emerge from his office. The receptionist, a big-haired redhead named Mandy, busied herself with the task of opening the daily mail. When Parker finally strolled out, I stood up to greet him. He wasn't exactly the repulsive monster I'd prepared myself for. His manner was mild and pleasant. His blond hair was recently trimmed and neatly styled. He was tall and muscular and dressed in an expensive-looking suit with a colorful tie. The only jewelry he wore was a Rolex watch, which he'd managed to check twice before he acknowledged my presence. His face was tanned, I assumed from hours on the golf course, courting potential clients. He didn't look like a killer. But neither had Ted Bundy.

"Hello, Mr. Parker," I said, holding my hand out to shake his. "Spencer Davis told me you were looking for an experienced systems person for installations and user training."

Bradley Parker studied me briefly, then smiled and shook my hand. "Spencer Davis?" he replied, looking a bit confused.

"Yes. He met you at the computer show up in Sacramento. Cal Expo. You offered him a job," I explained.

The floodgates of remembrance opened. "Right. Right. I remember him. Bright kid. Wish I could've talked him out of that State job. He could be a real asset."

I smiled and handed him my résumé. "He taught me everything I know—about computers, that is."

Parker took the résumé and glanced over it quickly. "Unfortunately, I've already filled the position. Last week. Very competent fellow."

The wind in my sails suddenly died. I hadn't considered the possibility that I'd strike out. I didn't have a backup plan. How could I have been so confident that I'd just walk into the job? I'd become very naïve since leaving the world of high tech. There's more competition out there now. Kids right out of school are writing their own tickets. Never mind that they have no business experience and will likely make mistakes that cost clients thousands, or maybe even millions of dollars. They're the computer-game generation, able to navigate an electronic maze filled with fire-breathing monsters and flying creatures so deadly they kill on contact. They can collect all the gold coins, outmaneuver the mutant attackers, and win the game, but they don't understand the ramifications of providing inaccurate information to decisionmakers of multimillion-dollar companies.

I frowned and nodded. "I see," I said, turning to leave.

Mandy caught his attention before he returned to his office. "Bradley, don't forget you're supposed to meet Pamela for lunch."

I slowly gathered my purse and briefcase, stalling my exit to listen to the exchange between Parker and Mandy.

Parker checked his watch. "Today? I've got a lunch appointment with—what's his name—you know, the guy with the white BMW."

"Mr. Axtell. You want me to call Pamela and cancel?" Mandy asked.

Parker waved his hand in the air as if he were parting the Red Sea. "Yeah. We can go over the guest list some other time. I don't know why she needs me to be involved in every little detail of this wedding," he complained.

My ears perked up at the mention of a wedding.

"Has Pamela gotten a dress yet?" Mandy asked.

Parker shook his head and blew out a sigh of disgust. "You kidding? She hasn't even thought about it. I told her Vegas was the way to go, but she wouldn't hear of it. When the day comes and she's not ready, she won't have a choice."

I couldn't believe my ears. *You can bet the girl has thought about a dress,* I said to myself. *From the day she was twelve years old, she's thought about the dress she'd wear on her wedding day.* I dropped my purse and spilled all the contents on the floor, slowly gathering the items and neatly placing them back, one by one.

Parker returned to his office as Mandy dialed the phone. She tapped a pencil on her desk as she waited for an answer. She pushed the tip of her long, red, false fingernail against the hook and pressed some more buttons. "I can't reach Pamela at home," she said into the receiver. "Want me to call the restaurant and leave a message for her? Okay. It was Tucker's Grille, right?"

I made a mental note. Tucker's Grille was about fifteen minutes away. I finally got my stuff together and pushed my way out of the building.

I parked in the restaurant lot with a view to the front entrance and watched as patrons entered and exited. I waited until I saw a woman walk in alone. I didn't give her too much notice because she was very young—too young to be marrying Bradley Parker. When she walked out less than two minutes later with a very frustrated look on her face, I changed my tune. As she marched toward her car she looked as though she'd like to punch out a window or break a few antennas.

I grabbed my cell phone, purse, and the dress and piled out of the Ford. I hoisted my purse on my shoulder, held the dress hanger over my head to keep it from touching the ground, and pressed the cell phone to my ear, trying to summon the most aggravated voice I could. "What? I'm already here at the restaurant," I blurted into the phone, loud enough for the approaching woman to hear. She glanced at me and immediately noticed the dress I held over my head. "But I wanted to show you the dress. Why can't you make it?" I continued to whine into the phone. The woman paused and gave me a concerned glance. I acknowledged her sympathy and continued with my one-sided argument. "It just would have been nice if you could have let me know a little sooner, that's all. You're not going to do this to me on the wedding day, are you?" I said, laying it on thick. "Fine. 'Bye." I said, flipping the phone off. I struggled to open my purse when the woman offered to help.

"Here. Can I help? I'll hold the dress for you," she offered, taking the hanger from me.

"Thanks," I said, handing the dress over so I could drop the phone in my purse. "I'm so angry. Sorry you had to hear all the gory details," I said.

She smiled. "That's okay. We have more in common than you know. My fiancé stood me up today, too." She admired the dress through the clear plastic. "This is gorgeous. Where'd you get it?" she asked.

That was all it took. We'd both been stood up at the last minute by our inconsiderate fiancés, we were both planning weddings, and we were suddenly and unexpectedly free for lunch.

## Chapter Eight

Pamela Smythe met Bradley Parker at the bank where she worked as a teller. She spilled all the details of their whirlwind courtship over appetizers at Tucker's Grille.

Her youthful innocence amused me. I guessed her age to be around twenty-five. She had short blond hair and big blue eyes that batted like butterfly wings. Her petite figure, though too short for her to be a model, complimented her expensive designer outfit. If she was wearing makeup, I couldn't tell. Her complexion was clear and smooth and slightly flushed. Her dainty hands boasted a French manicure, and if I were a betting woman, I'd say her toes were done the same way.

Pamela didn't classify her thoughts into compartments. She didn't separate intimate personal details from the subjects more commonly considered safe, like the weather. She was an open book, withholding nothing, even from me, a perfect stranger. There was no filtering of thoughts going on before she allowed them to flow freely from her lips. I would call her childlike in that regard. She obviously had never been betrayed.

For every personal anecdote she conveyed about first kisses and long romantic walks on the beach with Bradley, I'd return some comment about Craig's shoe size or the color of his hair. I knew in my heart that I'd found the greatest guy in the world, but I didn't want to boast about it. I just knew the instant I felt the least bit smug, somehow I'd lose every good thing that Craig had brought to my life. Lucky. That's what I felt—lucky that the years of empty searching were over. My mind drifted for a moment and I had to snap myself back to reality. Pamela was chatting away and I'd missed her last sentence. I blinked my eyes and refocused on the conversation.

She informed me that her wedding was to take place in three weeks, and she was nowhere near ready. I already knew this, of course, but I feigned total astonishment. Nothing would make me happier than to upset Bradley Parker's underhanded scheme to squash her wedding-day dream by dragging her off to Las Vegas.

I watched her covet the dress I'd hung from a hook on the end of our booth and I suddenly had the unfamiliar feeling of being a big sister. I found the thought of Bradley Parker subjecting her to the same ordeal he'd put Diane through almost unbearable. I wanted to grab her and shake her and tell her what a terrible mistake she'd be making by marrying such an awful man. Tact forced me to keep my mouth closed. After all, what if I was wrong about Bradley? Maybe he didn't kill Diane. Maybe he was really a nice guy. Maybe he was just misunderstood. Maybe the Earth is flat.

"You know, I could help you get ready for your wedding," I offered. "I have the time and you certainly seem to need the help."

Pamela breathed out a heavy sigh of relief. "Would you? I'd be so grateful."

I smiled and nodded. "I'd be happy to. It'll be fun. We should start by finding a dress right away. After lunch, I'll take you to Ann Marie's. That's where I got mine."

For a moment, I thought Pamela was going to cry. "That would be wonderful."

I removed a small notepad from my purse. "Let's make a list of what you still need to do before the wedding." I clicked the end of a ballpoint pen and waited, poised and ready to write.

She studied the ceiling. "Let's see. I guess I should have some flowers," she said.

I raised my eyebrows and proceeded to write.

"Do you know a good photographer?" she asked.

"You haven't found a photographer?" I marveled.

"No. Is that bad?" she asked.

"Three weeks? I don't know if we'll find a reputable one on that short notice. Is money an issue?"

Pamela shook her head. "No. Bradley's paying for the whole wedding. He said to just send him the bills."

"Wow. Guess your folks must be relieved," I said.

Pamela frowned. "My parents died when I was sixteen. I don't have any other family. Bradley's all I have. He's my family now."

My heart sank. *This poor kid,* I thought. I didn't know what to say. I gave her the most sympathetic look I could. I'm sure she thought it was in response to the fact that she'd lost her parents, but if I had to be honest, it was really because she was about to chain herself to Bradley Parker.

She shook the brief moment of sorrow off. "Don't be sad. I'm happy. I'm in love with the most wonderful man in the world, and in three weeks, I'm going to have the most beautiful wedding ever."

I put the pen back to the paper and made a note. "I'll check with my photographer. Maybe he has an opening, or knows someone who might be available. What else?"

The waitress brought our food. I cleared a spot for my salad and asked for a refill of my water. Pamela spread a pat of butter on a warm roll. "A caterer would be a good idea. At first, I was just going to have a cake reception, but if we have an evening wedding, we should probably feed the guests."

I set my fork down. "You don't know if you're having an evening wedding?" I asked.

"I haven't decided."

"You mean you don't have the church reserved?" I asked, sounding more like a mother than a helpful acquaintance.

"Oh, no. Bradley doesn't want a church wedding," she replied.

*Right. Someplace where he won't be struck down by lightning the second he steps foot in the place,* I thought. I set the pen down on the table. "Maybe we should take a different approach. What *have* you taken care of, so far?"

Pamela appeared slightly injured. "I'm sorry. I'm really embarrassed. I'm just horrible at planning and organizing. It's one of those things that, if you don't learn by a certain age, you never will."

I felt like a heel. This poor girl hadn't developed the callused scars around her heart that life tends to create, and I'd managed to unwittingly hurt her feelings. "It's okay,

Pamela. Everything will work out. Have you considered a Nevada wedding? Not Vegas, but maybe Lake Tahoe?"

She shot me a horrified look, her eyes as big as saucers. "No. I refuse to get married next to a slot machine."

I could tell she was adamant and there was no point explaining that it wouldn't have to be the way she imagined it, marching down an aisle flanked by one-armed bandits to a minister who doubled as a blackjack dealer. I picked up my pen. "Okay, then we better get busy. Tell me what we have to work with."

"I have reserved the day at Bay Vista. Have you seen it? It's spectacular. We'll have the entire Pacific Ocean as a backdrop."

I jotted it down and nodded with approval. "Good."

"And I have a Justice of the Peace arranged. He's available any time that day. I just need to let him know the time."

I flipped the page on my notebook and started on a fresh sheet. "Okay. Here's what we still need to do. Invitations?" I looked at her with raised eyebrows. She nodded. I wrote it down. "Flowers. Photographer. I think you should go for the cake reception and forego the caterer."

"Okay," she agreed.

"Cake. Chairs for the guests. How many?" I asked.

"About a hundred."

"One hundred chairs. A table for the cake. Punch. Wine?"

"Champagne," she said decisively.

"Champagne. Glasses. Plates. Forks. Do you like chocolate-covered strawberries?" I asked.

Pamela rolled her eyes. "I love them."

"Good. Me too. They'll go great with the champagne."

I continued adding to the list when a thought popped into my head. "You'll need favors for the guests. You know what would be really cool? Bubbles. It's outdoors. It's perfect. What do you think?"

Pamela giggled. "Bubbles? Like what I played with as a kid?"

"Yeah. They're really popular for weddings now. Rice makes such a mess and people slip and fall all the time on it," I explained, repeating what I'd learned when looking for favors for my own day of bliss.

"I like it. Yeah. Bubbles," she said, beaming.

I wrote it down. "Good. Let's go find a dress."

Ann Marie's had one dress in the entire store that fit Pamela perfectly, needing no alterations at all. Luckily, it also made her look like a princess. She actually cried when she saw herself in the mirror. I warned her to stop or she'd get mascara on the white satin. My suspicions were confirmed when she told me she wasn't wearing any mascara. She was a natural beauty. Ann Marie's would have it pressed and ready to pick up in a week.

Pamela invited me to dinner at Bradley's house that evening so we could go over the guest list. I offered to print the invitations and envelopes with my computer to save time.

"Oh, and be sure to bring Craig along. I'm dying to meet him," Pamela said.

I smiled and agreed to extend the invitation to him. I hoped she'd spend one evening with a truly decent man and realize the creature she was about to walk down the aisle with was nothing but a snake trying to pass himself off as a human being.

The dinner invitation was a stroke of luck. It would give me a chance to snoop around and see what I could find out about Diane. We drove around the La Jolla neighborhood, searching for the address Pamela gave me. The homes were gorgeous. Views of the Pacific were spectacular.

"Parker's business must be doing well for him to keep his home here," I said.

Craig pulled into the driveway and set the brake. "You're not kidding about that. These are some expensive places."

I wondered about the trouble with his business, mentioned in Diane's letter, and how he managed to recover so quickly.

Pamela answered the door and let us into the house. "Hi. Come on in. You must be Craig," she said, holding out her hand.

"Nice to meet you," Craig replied, shaking her hand.

She led us past the entry, where I picked up the scent of garlic cooking. We followed the wonderful smells through the living room and into the kitchen, where she was putting the final touches on a German chocolate cake.

"I love German chocolate cake. Can I help with anything?" I offered.

"Nope. Everything is just about ready, believe it or not. I can't plan a wedding, but I can cook like Emeril," Pamela boasted.

Bradley strolled into the kitchen carrying a brandy snifter half full of the amber liquid. Pamela flashed him a huge smile.

"This is Devonie and Craig, sweetie," Pamela said.

I put my hand to my chest and put on a look of total surprise. "Well, we meet again. What a coincidence. I didn't know you were engaged to Pamela."

Pamela gawked at the two of us. "You've met?" she asked.

"I applied for a job today with your fiancé's company."

"Wow. What a small world," Pamela said.

"Isn't it?" Craig replied. He winked at me. He didn't want to admit it, but he enjoyed this little game. He's sure in another life, he was some sort of James Bond spy.

Bradley forced a smile. "Hello," he said, regarding me with a look I would almost have called irritation. He offered a hand to Craig and shook it like a boy being forced to shake hands with his enemy after getting in trouble for fighting. He never offered to shake my hand. I guessed that was an honor only extended to other men, certainly not to women who threatened his underhanded schemes. I was sure Pamela had explained to him how I was going to help her with her wedding plans so she wouldn't have to resort to a Vegas wedding.

He turned his attention to Pamela. "How long till dinner?"

"Not long. Why don't you give Devonie and Craig a tour of the house while I put the finishing touches on this cake," she said.

We followed Bradley into the living room, where he stopped at the bar to refill his glass. "Drink? Brandy's my poison, but I can give you just about anything under the sun," he offered.

"No, thanks," I replied.

Craig shook his head. "I'll wait till dinner," he said.

The room was large and heavily furnished. There was too much furniture to comfortably walk around. The wall facing the ocean must have been mostly windows, but the curtains were drawn, and the room was a little too dark for my liking. I inspected the framed photos on the fireplace mantel. I recognized the two teenage boys from the pictures in Diane's purse. There were photos of Bradley and Pamela, but nothing that even indicated Diane had ever lived there. I supposed that could be understood. The new fiancé would not want reminders of the previous wife around, no matter how bad the relationship had been.

"Good-looking boys. Yours?" I commented, nodding toward the graduation pictures.

"Yeah. Both are at UCLA. Costing me a fortune," he complained.

*Why don't you just push them off a cliff and solve your problem?* The wheels began turning in my head, and I got down to the business at hand. "Does their mother help with their expenses?" I asked in an effort to bring up the subject of Diane.

Bradley frowned. "No. Their mother died last year."

"Oh, I'm so sorry. Was she ill?" I asked.

"Accident," he answered, then took a drink of brandy.

"Dinner!" Pamela called from the dining room.

"I haven't finished the tour yet," Bradley called back to her. She stepped into the living room.

"I'll finish the tour after dinner. Come on, before it gets cold," Pamela insisted.

We sat down at the heavy oak dining table and admired the spread she'd put out. A lovely salad, garlic mashed potatoes, Cornish game hens, and a bowl of steamed vegetables. Pamela wasn't exaggerating when she said she could cook.

"This is great," Craig said, grabbing a hen with the tongs and placing it on his dish. "You've outdone yourself."

"Wait till you've tasted it before you start throwing around compliments," Pamela replied.

"Anything that looks and smells this good has got to be delicious," Craig said. "But you're right, to give a true compliment, I've got to put it to the taste test." He sliced a piece of white meat from the hen and speared it with his fork. Pamela watched with anticipation as he placed it in his mouth. He chewed it twice, then rolled his eyes in ecstasy. "This is wonderful," he said, taking another bite.

"Thank you," Pamela said, blushing.

I scooped a spoonful of potatoes and handed the bowl to Bradley. "Your business must be doing pretty well to have hired the new guy," I said.

He took the bowl from me. "I'm keeping busy."

Pamela handed me the vegetables. "He's doing much better, now that the lawsuits are over with," she said.

Bradley shot an angry glare at Pamela, but it went unnoticed. She was busy filling her salad bowl.

"Lawsuits?" I asked.

"Yeah. Over that crazy Voltage program. What a fiasco," Pamela said.

Bradley continued to fire daggers at her, but she had yet to look his direction.

"Voltage? I think I read something about that in *Computer World*," I said, trying to keep the conversation alive on the subject.

Bradley finally decided to speak up before Pamela had a chance to spill any more information. "I was a VAR for the company who sold the Voltage software."

"VAR?" I asked.

"Value added reseller," he explained. "I arranged demos

and set up meetings for clients who had a need for that particular type of software."

"Voltage? What's it used for?" Craig asked.

"It's sort of an ERP system for power plants. Handles resource planning, costing, forecasting, inventory, the whole enterprise," he explained.

"Except that it didn't work," Pamela interjected.

I could tell by the irritated look on Bradley's face that his patience with Pamela's comments was growing thin. He chose his words slowly and carefully. "The software didn't consistently perform as advertised, periodically producing erroneous results that were not immediately recognized."

I digested this statement. "The software didn't provide an auditing method?" I asked.

Bradley frowned. "The package didn't come with any reports. That was up to the client to develop, since each individual company had unique reporting needs. The database design was complicated, to say the least, with over seven hundred tables. Redundant data in multiple tables was sometimes conflicting, due to a failure to properly roll-back all transactions when there was a problem. It's the most de-normalized database design I've ever seen. The package relied heavily on triggers to update tables, especially in the inventory module, which caused more problems because of the rollback issue," he explained.

I cringed as he described problems caused by programming practices that should never have been implemented in a commercially available package—especially one with a price tag in the millions of dollars. The computer lingo went over Pamela's head, but the fact that she knew the software didn't work meant that Bradley had probably put it to her in simpler terms some time before that night.

"So, because you were a reseller, you were named in the lawsuits?" Craig guessed.

"Exactly. I no longer endorse the software, but the damage had been done," he said.

I glanced around the expensively furnished house. He was obviously still quite solvent. "You must have fared well in the suit," I noted.

"Oh, they settled out of court," Pamela reported.

I noticed Bradley's fist clench. He aimed his stare at Pamela, then picked up his dinner plate and shoved it toward her. "This has gotten cold. It needs to be heated up," he said.

"Certainly, sweetie. I'll just pop it in the microwave for a few seconds," she replied. I gaped as I watched her carry it, with a smile, into the kitchen.

Craig caught my expression and touched my leg under the table. "Can you pass the butter please, honey?" he asked, diverting my attention and helping me to maintain some self-control.

It would take every ounce of restraint I could muster to keep from giving Bradley a piece of my mind. I bit my tongue and continued eating. "You settled out of court? Must have been expensive," I pried.

"I survived," he said, taking another drink.

Pamela returned from the kitchen. "The insurance money helped," she said, placing the warmed dinner plate in front of him.

My ears perked up. "Insurance? Do you have some sort of coverage for lawsuits?" I inquired.

Pamela opened her mouth to speak, but Bradley cut her off. "No. It was completely unrelated. Can we change the subject? Talking about it's giving me heartburn," he said.

Pamela patted his hand. "Certainly, sweetie." She sat back down in her seat and leaned over toward me. "It was from his late wife's insurance policy," she whispered, loud enough for all of us to hear.

I jumped when Bradley dropped his fork on his plate and stood up. He didn't touch another bite of his newly warmed dinner. He picked up his brandy. "I'm done. If you'll excuse me, I have some work to do," he said and stormed out of the dining room.

"Don't you want some cake, sweetie?" Pamela asked.

He didn't reply. We watched him disappear into his home office. Pamela turned to us. "I'm sorry about that. He's not usually like this, but I think all the talk about the lawsuit and his late wife must have upset him. You knew his first wife died?"

"He told us. How did it happen?" I asked.

"She fell off a cliff or drowned or something. He never talks about it," Pamela said. She started clearing the dinner plates from the table. "You ready for some cake?" she asked.

Craig stretched back and patted his stomach. "I'm stuffed, but in a little while, you'll have to hold me back from attacking that cake."

"Me, too. How about that tour of the house you promised, then I'll help you with these dishes. By then, I'll be ready for cake," I said.

Craig took my empty plate and placed it on top of his. He stood and helped Pamela clear the table. "The two of you will not touch a dirty dish tonight. A rule of the house I grew up in said the one who cooks the meal doesn't wash up afterward. Besides, you have wedding business to take care of. You go tour the house. I'll do the dishes."

Pamela looked at me with raised eyebrows. "Is this the same man you argued with over the phone at the restaurant today?"

I had failed to fill Craig in on that particular detail of how I'd managed to work my way into Bradley Parker's life, but he seemed to catch on.

I winked at him. "Actually, it turns out he had been trying to reach me all morning, but I hadn't turned my phone on. I owe him a huge apology. It was totally my fault," I said, looking very remorseful.

"No. I'm sure it was my fault," Craig responded, trying to say the right thing.

"No. Believe me, honey, it was my fault," I said, hoping he'd quit trying to accept responsibility for the make-believe argument he knew nothing about.

"Okay. Whatever you say," he said, smiling at me. "You have an apron, Pamela?"

Pamela handed him an apron and showed him where the scrubber brush was, then she led me off on the rest of the tour.

The house had four bedrooms plus the office, four bathrooms, a family room and living room, formal dining room, and breakfast nook adjoining the kitchen. The laundry room was just off the three-car garage. The master bedroom was enormous. I entered and my eyes immediately fixed on a gorgeous solid oak roll-top desk in the corner. "What a beautiful desk," I said, running my hand along the smooth wood.

Pamela frowned. "It was Diane's. He gave it to her for one of their wedding anniversaries. I'd like to move it out of here—bad memories, you know. He finally did allow me to pack up some of the clothes she left here when she moved out. I need to find a place to take it."

I nodded with acknowledgment. I glanced around the room and spotted a huge Jacuzzi tub through the door to the master bathroom. I entered the room and admired the marble tub. Frosted glass windows surrounded it. The fixtures were polished brass and matched the double sinks' faucets. "I'm afraid I'd never leave that tub once I got in," I said.

"I know. It's really relaxing," she replied.

My eyes stopped on the open door to an enormous walk-in closet. I stepped through the door and was mesmerized by the size of it. "Wow—you could hold a dance in here," I said.

"Isn't it great? There's room for everything," she said.

Two large plastic bags were piled in the corner, stuffed full of women's clothes. Those must have been the things Pamela said she'd packed up. I studied the boxes on the shelves. The one that caught my attention was a simple computer-paper box, with big, bold letters printed on the side: "Diane's things."

I brushed past Pamela, through the door, and back into the bedroom. I sat down at the roll-top desk and stroked the smooth wood again. "I've been wanting to get a wedding gift for Craig. He'd love this desk. If you think Bradley would be willing to part with it, I would like to buy it."

"That would solve my problem of wanting it out of here," Pamela noted.

"That's sort of what I was thinking," I said.

"I'll ask him," she said. She thought for a moment, then continued. "But not tonight. We don't want to discuss it in front of Craig. I'll call you tomorrow. Are you ready for some cake?"

"Definitely," I replied.

Pamela started out of the bedroom.

"I'll be right there. I just need to use your restroom," I said.

"Okay," she replied over her shoulder as she strolled down the hall.

I watched her until she disappeared around the corner, then slipped into the closet and switched on the light. The box was on a high shelf, but it wasn't out of my reach. I pulled it down, careful not to spill the contents on my head. I sat it in the middle of the floor and started removing the items stored inside. An assortment of bud vases, a paperweight, a framed diploma from UCLA with Diane's maiden name printed on it, a small spiral notebook, and a videotape labeled *Science Project*. I stuffed everything but the notebook and video into the box and hoisted it back on its shelf. I inspected my attire—a pair of khaki shorts and a striped cotton T-shirt with three-quarter-length sleeves. No place to tuck anything this bulky. I glanced around the closet. My eyes stopped on the two plastic bags. I quickly stuffed the video and notebook in one of them, under several layers of clothing. I opened the door and slipped back out of the closet. Bradley Parker stood in the middle of the bedroom with his arms folded across his chest and scrutinized me. I hoped I didn't have the same expression I used to get when my mom caught me eating spoonfuls of brown sugar out of the box. My heart skipped a beat, but I didn't blink. I smiled at him.

"I can't believe the size of that closet. I just had to get another look at it. What are the dimensions?" I asked, trying to sound as relaxed as I could even though my heart was racing and about to pound its way out of my chest.

He shrugged. "I'm not sure. I can get a tape measure," he offered in a tone that made it clear it would be a huge inconvenience for him.

"Oh, no. That's okay. I was just curious."

Bradley, Pamela, Craig, and I sat around the dining table and devoured the cake in silence. Whether it was my imagination or not, I felt Bradley's stare and was sure he was suspicious of me. I was uncomfortable and wanted to leave. Finally, Bradley shoved his chair out from the table and stood up, leaving his dirty plate for someone else to pick up.

"That was great, Pam. I'm going to back to my office to finish up some work." He turned his attention to Craig and me. "Good night. It's been a pleasure," he said, with all the sincerity of a snake.

"Good night," I replied, resisting an urge to jump across the table and knock him upside the head with his dirty dessert plate.

Craig stood and shook his hand one more time. "It was good to meet you," Craig said. Then he picked up all the dessert dishes and headed for the kitchen.

While Craig finished up the dishes, Pamela and I sat down at the table and went over her guest list. I gathered up all the names and slipped the list in my purse. I checked my watch. "You know, I have to drop off a bunch of stuff at the Goodwill station in the morning. I could take that stuff you've packed up and save you a trip," I offered.

Pamela smiled. "Would you? I'd really like to get it out of here so I can have room to put my things."

Craig helped me load the two large bags in the car. Pamela waved as we backed out of the driveway and headed toward home. Bradley never came out of his office to see us off. He had no idea we'd left his house with Diane's things.

## Chapter Nine

Craig set himself to the task of repairing my VCR, which had gone on the blink more than a month ago. I sat cross-legged on the sofa in the main salon of the *Plan C* and paged through the notebook I'd liberated from Bradley Parker's dancehall-sized closet. Diane's notes were sketchy and cryptic. She did manage to date the top of each page. The first few pages seemed to refer to a school-board meeting she must have covered. References to *PTA* and *irate teachers* were my biggest clue.

I gathered from the references to border collies, poodles, and basset hounds that the next few pages were about a dog show held at Dog Park last year.

She had five pages of notes regarding the grand opening of the new skateboard park south of La Jolla.

She also dedicated quite a lot of space to notes about new cameras recently installed at certain intersections to catch red-light runners. The cameras would photograph any cars running red lights and citations would be mailed to the registered owners of the vehicles in the photos. San Diego had installed quite a few of these cameras, much to the dismay of many of the lesser-skilled drivers in the crowded community.

The last page with any entries was dated May seventh. I rummaged through the stack of newspaper articles I'd printed regarding the discovery of Diane's body. May seventh was a Friday. The coroner estimated the date of her death to be May eighth. I studied her notebook again. The words on the page read: *Where did they get it? Where could they get it? SONGS?*

"You have a smaller screwdriver?" Craig asked.

His question brought me out of a semi-trance. "What? Oh, yeah. In the bathroom drawer, next to the toothpaste," I replied.

"Bathroom?"

"When you live on a boat, you find new and innovative ways to store things. I've tried several locations, and believe me, it's the most efficient place for it."

"I'm sure it is," he said, heading for the bathroom.

"Does the word songs mean anything to you?" I asked as he returned with the small Phillips screwdriver.

"Songs? Let's see. Yeah," he said, then began singing a love song in a voice I'd never heard before. He crooned as he continued working on the VCR.

I gazed at him. I'd never heard him sing before. His voice was magical. How could I not know this about him? Here I was, only a few weeks away from marrying him, and I didn't even know he had the voice of an angel. "Where'd you learn to sing like that?" I asked.

"My mom's Aretha Franklin."

I laughed at his matter-of-fact delivery and tossed a pillow at him. "She is not. Is that thing fixed yet?"

"Yep. Just let me put the cover back on."

"You missed your calling, you know," I said.

"What, as a TV repair man?"

"No. A singer. You've got a great voice."

"Gee, thanks, but I think I'll stick to medicine. I'm a little old to change careers now."

"Okay, but promise me you'll sing for me once in a while?"

"It's a deal." He snapped the cover back on the VCR and set it back in its original position on top of my TV. "There you go. Good as new, I hope."

I put the notebook down and picked up the videotape. I slipped it into the VCR and pressed the PLAY button.

The video opened on a closeup of a blackboard with the chalked words:

JOSH AND JEREMY LAWRENCE
SCIENCE PROJECT
MR. CLAYTON
APPLIED SCIENCE
LINCOLN HIGH

"Wow. It really works," Craig said.

"You seem surprised. I never doubted your ability."

"You should have. I've never seen the inside of a VCR before. But I couldn't have you thinking you're marrying a man who's totally useless around the house. Luckily, there was a broken piece of videotape stuck in it. Anyone could have figured it out."

"Well, you're my hero. Shh. Let's watch."

The camera focused on two boys standing behind a table in a garage or workshop. The boys looked to be about fifteen or sixteen years old. One was thin and pale—a goth. His face was ivory white, his long, stringy hair dyed coal black. He wore tight black pants and a black turtleneck with some sort of silver symbol hanging from a chain around his neck. The other boy was equally as thin, but more colorful. His spiky hair stood straight up and was dyed a rainbow of colors. He had pierced his eyebrow and a small gold ring hung just over the corner of his right eye. He had a tattoo of a lizard wrapped around his upper left arm. He wore a T-shirt with the sleeves cut off and baggy pants that hung two inches lower than the top of his boxer shorts.

On the table in front of the boys was a strange cylindrical object. It was about the size of a large fire extinguisher and sort of resembled one. The goth boy began speaking, and I turned up the volume on my television. He proceeded to explain that the device was a bomb he and his brother had built. I sat up straight and adjusted the volume again. They were very proud of themselves. They had gotten all the information they needed to build the bomb from the Internet. It was easy, they boasted. The rainbow-haired boy then began explaining the chain of events in a nuclear reaction.

"Nuclear?" I whispered, afraid of what I was witnessing. Craig's concerned eyes met mine.

The goth boy continued by explaining that the twenty pounds of plutonium they'd used for the bomb could result in a thirty-five-kiloton blast, equivalent to seventy million pounds of TNT. I tried to fathom seventy million pounds of *anything*, let alone TNT.

The boys concluded their presentation with a request to their teacher: "Hope we get an A, Mr. Clayton."

Craig made me promise I'd take the tape to Sam Wright. I assured him I would. He held me and looked straight into my eyes. "I mean it. This is getting a little too weird. I'm worried about you. Give the tape to Detective Wright and let him handle it."

I smiled up at him and closed my eyes. "I'll give him the tape. Don't worry. I'll be fine."

I stood in the office of Lincoln High School and waited for the woman to give me directions to Mr. Clayton's classroom. She explained that he had a first-period class, and I'd have to wait until the bell rang before I could interrupt him.

I stood outside the door marked 7 in the science building and waited for the bell to ring. When it did, fifty teenagers blasted through the door, nearly knocking me down. When it appeared safe to proceed, I entered the classroom. Mr. Clayton was busy cleaning the chalkboard.

"Mr. Clayton?" I asked.

Surprised, he turned. "Yes? Can I help you?" he replied.

"I have a video made by a couple of your students. I wonder if you could take a look at it and give me your thoughts?" I asked.

He checked his watch. "I don't have a class this period. I guess I have time. Is it long?"

"About twenty minutes," I said.

Baxter Clayton was visibly disturbed by what he'd seen. When the tape concluded, he pressed the REWIND button and shook his head. "Where did you get this?" he asked.

"You mean you've never seen it?"

"No. Are you kidding? Those boys would be expelled, or better yet, locked up, if I'd ever seen it."

"It was in the personal items of a reporter for the *Union Tribune*," I explained.

"Where'd he get it, then?" Clayton asked.

"*She* isn't around to tell. She's deceased."

Clayton's face grew pale. He looked like he wanted to be sick.

"In your opinion, is this bomb for real? Do you think these boys have really built a nuclear device?" I asked, hoping for the best, but expecting the worst.

"Josh and Jeremy Lawrence are extremely bright boys. Everything they explained in the video was correct and complete. If they really have the plutonium, then there's no doubt they have a full-scale nuclear bomb," he answered.

"But how realistic is it that they could get their hands on plutonium? I mean, it's not something you can get at your local hardware store."

"I would hope they couldn't acquire it," he said.

"Even if they did, where could they have gotten it?" I asked.

"Only place that comes to mind is San Onofre," he replied.

"San Onofre?"

"Yeah. San Onofre Nuclear Generating Station. You know—SONGS," he explained.

I snapped my fingers. "Of course! SONGS. It's an acronym."

I explained to Baxter Clayton that I was going to turn the videotape over to the police but I wanted the boys' parents to view the video first. He was reluctant to give me the Lawrence family's address and would only give it to the police. I let Clayton use my cell phone to call the number for the San Diego police department. When he got through, I took the phone from him and asked to speak to Sam Wright. I explained to Sam that another clue had, in his own words, "miraculously landed in my lap," and that Baxter Clayton, a teacher at Lincoln High, was going to give him the address where he could pick it up.

"What are you talking about?" Sam demanded.

I ignored his request. "Here. This is Mr. Clayton. He's a science teacher," I said, then handed the phone to Baxter. "Just give him the address," I instructed.

Baxter put the phone up to his ear. He read the address from a paper he'd pulled from a file in his desk. I wrote it down as he read. He handed the phone back to me.

"Did you get that?" I asked.

"Yeah. What's this about?" he demanded again.

"I'll fill you in before you get there. Can you meet me there tonight? Six-thirty?"

I visualized the color of his face in my mind. By now, I was sure it was deep red, with his jaw clenched so tight a crowbar couldn't pry it open. "You are on thin ice, you know," he hissed into the phone.

"I know, but you're gonna flip when you see what I've got," I assured him.

"I'll flip you—right on your ear," he promised.

"Just meet me there. Okay?"

"I'll be there, but you better find yourself a bodyguard, 'cause I'm gonna snap every bone in your scrawny little neck when I get a hold of you."

"Where'd you go to charm school?" I asked.

The line went dead. He hung up on me. Part of me wondered if I should take his threat seriously. I took the video from the VCR and thanked Baxter Clayton for his help.

At five, I called Sam and gave him the details of what was on the tape. He insisted that I bring it to him at the station, but I refused. I would gladly hand it over to him, but only at the Lawrence household. I knew if I gave it to him at the station, he'd take it and that would be the last I'd ever hear about it. He'd never tell me anything. Before he hung up he grumbled something about interfering with an investigation, withholding evidence, and an arrest warrant. I didn't take him seriously. Surely by now, I'd gotten on his good side.

When I arrived at the address Clayton had given us, Sam's car was already parked at the curb. I pulled in behind him and could see he was still sitting inside. A gold Mercedes pulled into the driveway of the home we were headed for, then into the garage. The automatic door closed behind it. I took a deep breath and opened my door. I didn't head for Sam's car. Instead, I went right for the front door of the house. Sam jumped out of his car and called me. I waved for him to follow me.

"Get over here!" he demanded.

I ignored his command and waved him over again. Then I rang the doorbell. Sam raced up the walk and reached me just as the door opened.

Mrs. Lawrence was confused and concerned about why this police officer and woman wanted to see her sons. She was relieved when her husband entered from the garage. She turned the whole matter over to him. He set his brief-case down and walked into the living room.

"What's this about?" he asked.

I handed the video to Sam.

Sam glared at me. If looks could kill, I'd be on a slab in the morgue. I'd put him in a very precarious position, but I didn't want to be left out of the loop.

Sam addressed Mr. Lawrence. "This is a video your sons produced, apparently as a project for school. I'd like to talk to them about it," Sam said.

"And you're from the police?" Mr. Lawrence asked. He loosened his expensive tie and removed his jacket, throwing it across the back of a leather recliner.

"I am, yes. Detective Wright," Sam said, showing him his badge.

"What's on the tape?" Lawrence asked.

"We'll all watch it together, if you don't mind. You'll be interested, I'm sure," Sam said.

Lawrence nodded toward his wife. "The boys around?" he asked.

She frowned. "I don't know. They may have gone out to get a pizza. They said something about being hungry when I got home from work."

"Well, go see," he instructed her. She gave him a concerned look, then left the room.

The home was exceptionally clean and neat for a household with teenagers and two working parents. It looked almost unlived-in. The only sign of human life was Mr. Lawrence's jacket tossed over the back of the recliner. I contemplated that for a while, then decided either Mrs. Lawrence was an overachiever, or she had a housekeeper.

When she returned without the boys, Lawrence told her to check the backyard. Again, she flashed him a concerned, questioning look, then disappeared through a door. Minutes later, she returned with the two boys from the video on her heels.

Josh and Jeremy looked very much the same as they did on the video. Josh, the older son, was still pale with jet-black locks, skin-tight black clothes, and silver symbols hanging from the chain around his neck. Jeremy had apparently settled on a single color for his hair since the video was made. Pink. Hot pink. His body piercing had been expanded to include rows of earrings down both ears, and a stud in his tongue. The lizard tattoo was concealed under the sleeves of his oversized T-shirt.

The boys plopped down on the sofa. Jeremy glanced at the faces around the room. "What's up?" he finally asked, wondering who the strangers were.

Sam asked to play the video. We all watched together. I studied the boys' reactions. They were not concerned in the least. Mr. Lawrence, on the other hand, was sweating profusely. Mrs. Lawrence gaped at the television, unable to form a coherent sentence. Sam's eyes were glued to the screen. Even though I'd prepared him, he still seemed to be surprised by the tape. When it was over, the boys were smiling.

Jeremy scooted to the edge of his seat. "Cool. Where'd you guys get it? Someone stole it out of my locker before we could turn it in to Mr. Clayton," he informed us.

I pictured a juvenile thief, breaking into lockers and taking anything that looked interesting. When he saw what was on the tape, he must have developed something of a conscience and mailed it to the newspaper in hopes of exposing the Lawrence boys.

Sam shot a cold, hard stare at Jeremy. "We're not here to return stolen property. It's illegal to possess plutonium.

If we're to believe this video is for real, I want to know where you got it."

Jeremy laughed. "Oh, man. Mike's dad has a bunch of it in his garage. We just—"

"Shut up, Jeremy," Josh hissed.

Jeremy frowned at his brother. "But—"

Mr. Lawrence stood up. "He's right. Shut up. I don't want to hear a word out of either of you."

"Karl," Mrs. Lawrence snapped. She'd finally managed to regain her voice.

"Go call Stan. Now!" he ordered his wife.

"Stan? Oh, Karl. What's happening?"

"Just do it! I won't discuss this any more without talking to my lawyer first."

Then the senior Lawrence marched over to his youngest son and lifted the sleeve of his T-shirt, exposing the evil-looking tattoo. "When did you do this?"

I gawked at the scene. The boy had a large tattoo on a part of his body that couldn't have been concealed twenty-four hours a day, and his father had been oblivious to it for at least a year. On top of that, why was Mr. Lawrence suddenly concerned about a tattoo when he'd apparently ignored the pink hair and mutilated ears, eyebrows, and tongue? Had he not noticed the bizarre appearance of his sons before? The answer was clear. He didn't pay enough attention to know they were building nuclear bombs in the garage.

And what about Mrs. Lawrence? Was she too concerned with her career to pay attention to her family? I often wonder why people have children they obviously are not interested in. They think it's a right, when in truth, it's a responsibility. It's like people who get puppies, then abandon them in the backyard, or take them to the pound after they grow up because they're not cute or entertaining anymore. Maybe if every parent were accountable for the actions of their children, they'd take a more active role in making sure they produced decent human beings, instead of letting the *village* create potential monsters.

"Do you still have this bomb?" Sam asked.

Karl Lawrence shoved his pointed finger in both boys' faces. "Don't say a word," he ordered.

Sam raged. "I can haul them both downtown and make life miserable."

"Do it, and you'll be hit with the biggest lawsuit your department has ever seen," Karl Lawrence shot back.

"On what grounds?" Sam growled.

"Harassment. Minors. No evidence. All you have is a video and it might all be fiction," Lawrence replied.

Sam's color turned deeper red. I was concerned he might actually lose control and punch Mr. Lawrence in the stomach.

I decided to get involved in the conversation. "I was talking to Mr. Clayton at your school today. He watched the video. He told me you boys are very bright—almost genius. His concern was that your intelligence is not being channeled in a positive direction. He also explained that the bomb you built is exactly what you claim—seventy million pounds of dynamite—but the manner in which you put it together makes it very unstable. It's extremely susceptible to barometric changes and sensitive to fluctuations in temperature and humidity." He, of course, said nothing of the sort, but I thought I could put a scare into one or both of the boys, or maybe even the mother.

Mrs. Lawrence shuddered. "Karl?" she cried.

The boys exchanged glances with each other.

"If you boys are as smart as Mr. Clayton says, then you realize how dangerous it is to have that thing anywhere within miles of here. Are you that smart?" I asked.

The previously cocky Jeremy had a change of heart. Tears began streaming down his face. "It's in the garage!" he blurted before his father could shut him up.

Sam called for the bomb squad. Within minutes, cars with flashing lights and squawking radios surrounded the house.

When the bomb experts finally appeared with the device, their report to Sam was clear. It was for real. The boys had actually built a nuclear device capable of destroying most of the city.

After the nuclear device had been removed and a string of yellow crime-scene tape put up around the house, Sam took me by the arm and led me to his car.

"Give me your keys," he said.

I looked at him quizzically. "What for?"

"So I can have one of the officers take your vehicle to the impound lot."

"What? Why?" I insisted.

"Because you're coming with me to the lockup."

"Lockup?" I had the same sinking feeling I'd gotten the first time my mother made good on her promise to spank me just as soon as we got home if I didn't stop doing gymnastics in the backseat of the car.

Sam hauled me to the police station, filled out an arrest report, had me fingerprinted, and locked me in a holding cell. Three hours later, he returned, yanked me out of the cell, and told me all charges were dropped and I could go home. He handed me my keys and pointed me toward the door.

I was beyond boiling mad. "How much did this little display of macho authority cost the taxpayers?" I snarled.

He drove his eyebrows together and shoved his finger at my face. "Not as much as it will the next time, 'cause if it happens again. I'm throwing the book at you. It won't be a little slap on the wrist. You'll do real time. Don't you ever withhold evidence and put me in a position the way you did today. Got it?"

I swallowed hard and nodded my head. My mother's tactic worked. I never did another somersault in a car again. Only time would tell if Sam's punishment would stick.

## Chapter Ten

I cursed under my breath when I skinned my knuckles trying to loosen the oil drain plug on the Explorer. As I lay on my back under the vehicle, I watched the tires of Craig's Lexus roll into the driveway. I saw his feet land on the pavement and stroll over to where I was working.

"What are you doing?" he asked, addressing my bare legs and deck shoe–attired feet, which were the only parts of my body exposed from under the Sunkist-mobile.

"Changing the oil," I replied. "Hope you don't mind me doing it in your driveway. There's not a good place at the marina for me to work on it."

He squatted down and peered at me. "Why?" he asked.

I continued loosening the bolt as I explained. "My dad always told me to use synthetic oil in my cars. Said it would make the engine last longer."

He chuckled. "No. I mean why are you doing it yourself? You can take it down to Speedy Oil and have it done in ten minutes."

"Why would I want to pay someone to do something I can do myself?" I asked. I scrambled to get the oil pan positioned under the stream of thick, black oil that poured out of the drain I'd just opened. "Shoot," I grumbled after I accidentally dropped the plug in the pan of dirty oil. My knuckle stung where'd I'd peeled the skin off when the wrench slipped. I scooted myself out from under the vehicle and rose to my feet. I'd had the foresight to wear an old T-shirt, on its way to the ragbag, but hadn't intended to ruin the denim shorts. I grimaced at the large oil stain just below the right pocket.

Craig disregarded the greasy mess I was, and wrapped his arms around me. "You're right. Why would you deny yourself this pleasure?" He kissed my forehead, which was probably the only spot on my entire upper body that wasn't covered in grease.

I gazed up at this ever-patient man I'd been so fortunate to find and smiled at him. "Plus, I'm saving at least thirty dollars," I added.

"Well, there you go. You're having an enjoyable experience, and you're saving yourself the cost of a new pair of shorts and a Sea World T-shirt."

I let out an embarrassed laugh. "You're right. Next time, I'll take it to the shop. It's just such a habit to try to save money."

He winked at me. "Are you about done? I'll fix us some dinner," he offered.

"Just about. I'll get cleaned up and give you a hand."

"Did you give the tape to Detective Wright?" he asked.

I bit my lip and wondered how much of my experiences that day I dared to reveal. I decided the truth was always the best approach, but that didn't mean the truth all at once.

"Yes," I said and left it at that. Someday, I'd tell him the rest, but I didn't want him to worry unnecessarily.

We sat on the back deck and dined on prawns Craig had grilled on the barbecue. We watched neighbors' boats setting out from their docks toward the open sea. Craig poured us each a glass of white wine.

"What did Detective Wright say about the video?" he asked.

"Not much. One of the boys told us they'd gotten the plutonium from the garage of someone named Mike. I offered to go over to the high school and search through the yearbooks for all the boys with that name."

"Us? You went with him to talk to the boys?" Craig questioned.

Oops. I'd let that slip. There was no way out. I'd have to tell him the whole story. He listened in silence as I described my day, finishing up with my three-hour stay at the police station in a holding cell.

Craig just shook his head and let out a chuckle. "I'm marrying a grown-up Nancy Drew."

I relaxed and joined in his amusement. "Anyhow, he told me if I set one foot in that school, he'd personally lock me up and feed the key to his neighbor's Rottweiler."

"And you let that stop you?"

"I learned my lesson. He's not opposed to me helping, as long as I don't put him a position like I did today," I said, knowing full well that the man would keep his promise the next time. The sun had moved so that I was no longer in the shade of the table's umbrella. I repositioned my chair closer to Craig. "I've been thinking, and I'm definitely going to hyphenate."

"Hyphenate?" he asked.

"Yeah. You know. Devonie Lace-Matthews. What do you think?"

"Oh. Right. Lace-Matthews. Sounds good," he said, easily taking the new course of conversation in stride.

"A lot of women are doing that now, you know," I said, almost as if I were defending my decision.

Craig nodded. "I know. Makes sense. I can't blame women today for not wanting to give up their identity. You've got a mind of your own."

I watched the sails fill on a beautiful boat as it glided past the private dock Craig shared with his neighbor. "He never said anything about *you* not setting foot in the high school," I said, switching to the original subject.

Craig eyed me over his sunglasses. "We're back on the case now?"

I finished the last swallow of my wine. "We need to find out who Mike is. The last thing Diane wrote in her notebook had to do with that video. Maybe she'd uncovered something. Maybe she found out about the plutonium, and if she did, maybe it got her killed."

I waited in Craig's car while he went into the school to look through the current yearbook. It would be a tedious process and I felt guilty for asking him, but he wanted to help and it felt good to accept his aid. He returned with a list of twenty-nine names. We both stared at the list in silence, wondering what to do next.

"What's our next move?" he asked.

I scratched my head. "I didn't think there'd be this many. I guess the best thing would be to give the list to Sam. If

I tell him that I didn't go in the school, and if you're with me when I give it to him, maybe he'll go easy on me."

Craig started the car. "Then we're going to the police station?"

"Yeah. I think it's best."

"Mind if we drive by the infamous bomb house? I'm kind of curious," Craig said.

"Sure. Just take that street," I said, pointing toward Pearl Street. "That'll take us by the Lawrence house."

The deserted house was marked off with yellow tape all the way to the street. Anyone walking on the sidewalk would have to detour. Craig parked a couple of houses away and we both stepped to the sidewalk.

A little boy pedaling a tricycle rang his bell at us to warn us not to get in his way as he rolled along the sidewalk. We paused to let him pass. He stopped and studied us. I grinned at him. He was about five years old, wearing a green-and-white striped T-shirt and faded blue jeans with grass stains on both knees. He had a mass of curly red hair and a sprinkling of freckles across his nose. A large Band-Aid covered his left elbow.

"You can't go inside that yellow tape," he warned us. "The police will get you if you do. You might go to jail."

"Is that right?" Craig responded.

"Yep. My dad told me so," he said.

"Well, we for sure'll stay away from the yellow tape then," Craig assured him.

"That's good. What's your name?" he asked, pointing toward me.

"Devonie," I answered. "And this is Craig."

"Devonie? I never heard that name before. How come that's your name?"

" 'Cause that's what my parents named me. What's your name?"

"Mike," he said, smiling proudly.

I looked down the street at the rows of mailboxes. "Mike? That's a nice name. Do you live here?" I asked, pointing toward the house next to the Lawrences'.

"No. I live over there," he said, pointing toward a two-story, three houses down.

I squinted at the name on the mailbox. Campbell. "Is your name Mike Campbell?" I asked.

"Yep."

"That's a really neat name. Is your dad's name Mike Campbell, too?"

He shot me a look as if I'd just suggested something as stupid as naming a cat Rover. "No. His name's Ralph Campbell."

"Oh. That's a nice name, too," I told him.

A woman's voice called "Mike?" from the Campbell house, though she never stepped out the door to see what the little boy was up to.

"I gotta go," Mike said, as he did a U-turn and pedaled his trike down the sidewalk toward his house.

Craig and I exchanged glances.

"It's a long shot," he said.

"I know, but I've got a feeling," I said as I quickly got back into the car and pulled the phone out of my purse. Craig slid into the driver's seat.

I dialed information and asked for San Onofre Nuclear Generating Station. The operator put my call through and a receptionist answered.

"Would it be possible to speak with Ralph Campbell?" I requested.

"One moment, please," she replied.

A minute later, a man's voice came on the line. "This is Ralph Campbell."

I hung up. "Pay dirt," I said to Craig.

My next call was to Sam Wright.

"I found him," I blurted into the phone.

Sam was confused. "Found who?" he asked.

"Mike," I answered, excited.

"How?"

"He lives three houses down from the Lawrences. He's a five-year-old kid," I explained.

"Five? Just because the kid's name is Mike doesn't mean it's the Mike we're looking for. You know how many Mikes there are in the world?" he argued.

"Yeah. But how many live three houses down from the Lawrence boys and have a father who works at San Onofre Nuclear Generating Station?"

Sam was silent. I wondered if I lost the connection. "Did you hear me? I said—"

"I heard you," he interrupted. "Are you sure about this?"

"Yes. His name's Ralph Campbell. I just called SONGS and asked to talk to him. He's for real," I assured Sam.

"You'd better be, because I'm going to use the special circumstances and your statement to convince a judge to give me a search warrant. If you're wrong, I'll personally—"

"I know, I know. You'll lock me up and feed the key to your neighbor's Rottweiler."

"No. I'll feed *you* to my neighbor's Rottweiler. Got that?" he threatened.

I replayed the last ten minutes over in my mind. Yes, the boy's name was Mike. Yes, his father's name was

Ralph Campbell. Yes, he confirmed his name when I called him at the SONGS plant. How much trouble could I be in if I were wrong? How much trouble could Sam be in if I were wrong? "I got it. How soon can you get here?" I asked.

Sam must have had a friend at the courthouse. He had a search warrant in less than an hour. When he arrived, he insisted Craig and I stay in our car. We agreed to cooperate, to avoid another trip to the lockup, although I did ask Craig to turn the car around and get a little closer so I could watch.

Mrs. Campbell read the papers Sam handed her, gathered Mike up, and shooed him into the house. She spoke into a portable phone as she watched the proceedings from the front porch. I could see her face was troubled.

When Sam rolled up the garage door, Craig let out a low whistle. "That's a '46," he said, admiring the shiny car sitting on the concrete. "Convertible. Completely restored. Must be worth about eighty grand," Craig speculated.

I gawked at Craig. I had no idea he knew about such things. "Eighty grand? You sure?" I asked.

"Pretty sure. I've seen a few sold on that roadster auction show. Always amazes me how much people will pay for some of those old restored cars."

I shook my head and turned my attention back to the activity in front of the Campbell house.

The Hazmat team suited up and marched into the garage.

From my vantage, I could see two Harley-Davidson motorcycles and a pair of Wave Runners on a trailer. I gazed at the brand-new motor home sitting in the RV parking space next to the house.

"Expensive toys for a working man," I said. I wondered what Ralph Campbell's position at SONGS was, that he could afford these luxuries.

A red Corvette pulled into the driveway just as the leader of the Hazmat team emerged from the garage carrying what I assumed was a Geiger counter. Sam conversed with the heavily suited man, but I couldn't make out the words.

The man in the Corvette jumped out of his car and rushed up the driveway. "What are you doing?" he yelled. Sam grabbed him by the arm and stopped him from entering the garage. The Hazmat man pointed to some gauges on the contraption he held, and I could tell by the expression on Sam's face that it wasn't good news.

Sam handcuffed the Corvette man and loaded him into the back of a police car. Mrs. Campbell cried as she spoke frantically into her portable phone.

Craig drove us to the police station. I asked him to stop and let me out before he parked when I saw Sam escorting Ralph Campbell toward the door. He let me out and agreed to meet me inside. I trotted across the street after Sam. "Would you wait up?" I demanded.

He motioned for the other two officers with him to take the prisoner inside, then waited for me to catch up to him.

"Go home," he ordered.

"No!" I replied. "You wouldn't have that guy if it weren't for me. That *is* Ralph Campbell, isn't it?"

"Yes, it is. Thank you for your assistance. Now go home," he insisted.

"I absolutely will not. You owe me, Sam. I know you're going to question him. I want to hear what he has to say." I crossed my arms over my chest and glared at him through eyes that delivered my message. I was not going to take no for an answer.

I waited for Craig at the front desk, but he must have had trouble finding a parking spot. I left a message for him and followed Sam down a long corridor.

Ralph Campbell could not see me on the other side of the two-way mirror. He was informed of his rights and knew his lawyer was on the way, yet he opted not to remain silent.

Sam sat across from him at a table and took notes with his stubby pencil as he interrogated him.

"Where did you get the plutonium?" Sam asked.

"Work—but I didn't really steal it," Ralph answered.

"Whether you stole it or not isn't the issue, Mr. Campbell. It's illegal to possess plutonium. San Onofre never reported any thefts," Sam reminded him.

"Of course they never reported it. They never knew it was missing," Ralph pointed out.

"You want to expand on that?" Sam asked.

"I tried to tell them when they put that new computer system in three years ago, but no one would listen," Ralph said. The level of frustration in his voice rose with each word.

Sam continued taking notes. "Go on," he said.

"I told my boss there was something wrong with the numbers the new program was reporting. They were sometimes off by as much as a quarter pound. He told me to take care of it, so I called the people who wrote it," Ralph explained.

"Wait a minute. Slow down. What numbers?" Sam asked.

"The inventory output numbers. It kept saying we had produced less by-product material than we'd actually measured," Ralph continued.

"By-product material?" Sam questioned.

"Yeah. Plutonium. It's a by-product of the fission chain reaction," Ralph said.

"So you reported this as a problem?" Sam asked.

"I did. I called the vendor. They told me it looked like a calculation-rounding problem and that I should post an adjusting entry to correct the discrepancies. I told them there was no way the company would go for that."

"And what did they say?" Sam asked.

"They said they'd look into it and maybe correct it in a future release of the software, if it proved to be a serious enough problem."

Sam wrote furiously in his notepad. I sat on the edge of my seat and waited for him to ask the right question. Surely he would ask.

"So what did you do then?" Sam asked.

"I told my boss. He told me to take care of it. He didn't care how, but I was not to bother him with any more computer problems again. I tried to do what the vendor told me to do—post an adjusting entry to correct the errors. That just made it worse. The adjustment ended up being stuck in a phantom inventory location, and when I tried to get it out, it understated the original inventory even more. It was a nightmare." Ralph wiped his sweaty brow with his shirt-sleeve. "Since I couldn't make the computer number match the inventory, I decided to make the inventory agree with the computer. It was easier to smuggle plutonium out in my lunch pail every day than it was to get that computer to come up with the right number," he admitted.

I wanted to shout through the wall to get Sam's attention. "Ask him what the name of the software is," I whispered to myself, hoping the subliminal message would make it to Sam's conscious mind. I knew Ralph Campbell's attorney would be making an entrance soon and Ralph would be hushed up just as effectively as if he'd been gagged. I tip-toed over to the glass and meekly tapped on it. Sam stopped writing in his notebook and shot an irritated glance at the mirror. He looked at it for a moment, then continued writing. I tapped again. His jaw clenched.

"Excuse me," Sam said, as he shoved his chair away from the table and stormed out of the interrogation room.

*"What?"* he hissed, getting his face within three inches of mine.

"Ask him the name of the software," I said.

"Why?" he demanded.

"Can you just ask him, before his lawyer shows up and he stops singing like a bird? I'll explain later," I pleaded.

I pictured my delicate little neck in the clenches of Sam Wright's big hands. I think he had the same picture in mind. He took my arm and sat me back down in a chair. "Don't touch that glass again," he ordered, pointing his finger in my face.

I watched as Sam returned to his seat across from Ralph Campbell. He put his pencil back to the paper. "What was the name of the computer program?" he asked.

"It's called Voltage. That's V-O-L-T-A-G-E," he said, watching to make sure Sam spelled it correctly in his notes. "I even tried to get the newspaper to write about it, but—"

The door to the interrogation room burst open at that moment. A middle-aged man in tennis attire stormed in.

"Don't say another word, Ralph!" the newcomer exclaimed.

Sam stood up. "I take it you're Mr. Campbell's attorney?"

"That's right. What the heck do you think you're doing interrogating him without me here?" he demanded.

Sam smiled. "Mr. Campbell was informed of his rights. He volunteered the information freely."

Ralph watched the two men spar for a moment, then interrupted. "It's okay, Harv. He's right. I wanted to tell them."

Ralph's attorney was furious. "You'd better not say another word, Ralph. You have no idea what you could be getting yourself into. You have more than yourself to think about, you know. You have a wife and kid. You'd better listen to me before you open your mouth one more time," Harv instructed.

Ralph seemed shocked. Had he forgotten he had a wife and son? Didn't he know he could actually go to jail? He must have been concerned about who would take care of them if he went to prison. He looked at Sam. "Where are my wife and son?"

"We've evacuated your house until the Hazmat team determines it's safe. Your wife wanted me to tell you they'll be staying with your next-door neighbor tonight."

Ralph never said another word.

## Chapter Eleven

Sam marched me down the hall to his office and sat me in the chair opposite his desk. He rolled up his sleeves, reached into his drawer, and removed a bottle of aspirin.

"Okay. What's the significance of Voltage?" he demanded, popping two tablets into his mouth.

"Bradley Parker had a connection with Voltage. He was selling it for a while. That's what all those lawsuits against him were about," I explained.

Sam tapped his pencil on the desk. I could see the wheels turning in his head. "Okay. So if we find out Parker sold the program to SONGS, we may have a reason to take a closer look at him, especially if Diane found out about the lost plutonium inventory. Campbell did say he went to the paper. If she threatened to expose the program, Bradley would have been hit with yet another lawsuit."

I nodded in agreement. "There's an even bigger problem here, you do realize."

Sam waited for me to continue.

I reached across the desk, picked up his pencil, and started scribbling calculations on his notepad. "Ralph said they installed Voltage three years ago. Right?"

"Right," Sam agreed.

"And he said it lost as much as a quarter pound of plutonium with each transaction," I continued.

"Right," Sam repeated.

"He also said he removed plutonium every day," I said, as I did the math. "That's over two hundred and seventy-three pounds. We know the Lawrence boys took about twenty of it, so that leaves somewhere in the neighborhood of two hundred and fifty. Your Hazmat team recovered, what, fifty pounds from Campbell's garage?"

"Fifty-two point five pounds, exactly," Sam confirmed.

I circled a number on the notepad. "That leaves about two hundred pounds."

"Two hundred pounds of plutonium unaccounted for," Sam noted.

"Oh, it's accounted for, all right. It's in that new motor home, those fancy cars in Campbell's garage, the Harleys, all his expensive toys that he shouldn't be able to afford on his salary," I said.

"He's selling it," Sam concluded.

I nodded. "You bet he is."

Someone other than Ralph Campbell's attorney arranged bail, and he was released before Craig and I left the police station. Sam assured me every available resource would be digging up whatever there was to find on Campbell, and any connection he may have had with Bradley Parker. He sent me home and made me promise to stop playing Sherlock Holmes.

\*   \*   \*

Craig and I had a dinner date at Angelina's that night. As we drove to the restaurant, I gave him a rundown of Ralph Campbell's interrogation and my conversation with Sam. He listened intently until I finally had nothing left to report. By that time, we were at the restaurant and ready to be seated.

The waiter put us at a quiet table in the back corner of the dining room. Craig took a sip of wine and shook his head, chuckling. "Missing plutonium. Kids building nuclear bombs in their garage. Women being thrown off cliffs. You think we'll ever have a conversation about something as mundane as what to plant in the flower beds or what color to paint the kitchen?"

I laughed, kissed him on the cheek, and whispered in his ear, "Gladiolas in the flower beds and white on the kitchen walls."

A parade of restored 1930s vintage roadsters cruised down the boulevard past the restaurant. I admired them through the window. The last one had passed, but my gaze remained on the street, watching nothing in particular.

Craig noticed my blank stare. "What are you thinking about?" he asked.

I turned my attention back to him. "That car in Campbell's garage. If you're right about how much it's worth—"

Craig gave me an injured look. How could I doubt him?

I started over. "I know you're right about the car. And all that other expensive stuff he had. He's not the CEO at San Onofre. He can't be making that much money."

"I wonder what the going rate for plutonium is these days?" Craig pondered.

"I don't know, but I bet if his lawyer hadn't shown up, Ralph would have filled us in on the details."

"Sounds like Ralph's not the sharpest knife in the drawer," Craig commented.

"I don't think he's stupid. I think he's suffering from a guilty conscience. It's like he wanted to unload the heavy burden he's been carrying around. You know what they say about the truth."

"It'll set you free, except in this case, it'll probably buy seven years in the pen," Craig said.

I pushed a ravioli around my plate before I finally stabbed it with my fork. "Ralph wants to talk. I can tell," I said, then popped the cheese-stuffed pasta into my mouth.

Craig set his glass of wine down and gave me the same look my father gave me the day I announced I was considering dropping out of college to pursue a career as a commercial jingle singer. It wouldn't have been a bad choice for someone who could carry a tune.


When Craig dropped me off at home, I supposed he thought I would be staying there for the rest of the night. I guess I shouldn't have assumed that. He knew me too well. I couldn't get Ralph Campbell out of my head. He wanted to tell his story. His attorney shut him up, but I wondered how much convincing it would take to get him to open up again. Maybe he'd talk to me if I passed myself off as a reporter, trying to expose the mismanagement at San Onofre. I was sure he'd go directly to his wife and son when he was released. I remembered they were staying with the neighbor. I jumped into the Ford and headed for Ralph Campbell's neighborhood.

The house was dark and, like the Lawrences' house, completely surrounded by yellow crime-scene tape. Lights were on at both neighbors' houses. I watched the houses for a minute, wondering which was the temporary housing for the Campbell clan. I was about to take a chance on the gray-and-white two-story when I saw the garage door begin to roll up on the other neighbor's house. I cranked my head around and watched. I saw Ralph Campbell throw a duffel bag into the passenger seat of a blue Volvo, jump into the driver's seat, and back slowly out of the driveway.

"What are you up to, Ralph?" I whispered to myself as I started my engine and pulled out into the street behind the Volvo.

It looked to me like Ralph was on the move. He was on his way out of town. I stayed on his tail. He must have sensed he was being followed, because his driving became fast and erratic. He wove in and out of traffic, and I worked to keep up with him. I wanted to call Sam on my cell phone to let him know it looked like Ralph was trying to skip town, but I couldn't take my attention off the road long enough to make the call. We were well out of the congestion of the city, and Ralph was running like a scared rabbit. I was having a tough time keeping up with the car. His lights disappeared from view when he rounded a curve. I pushed the gas pedal to the floor and gripped the steering wheel tightly. I slowed down before I reached the curve to keep from rolling my short-wheel-based SUV. When I straightened out the wheel, Ralph's taillights came back into view. I pushed the accelerator to the floor.

My heart sank when the red lights at the railroad crossing started flashing and the bells began their alarm. Ralph had made it through before the crossing gates came down, but no such luck for me. I eased my foot down on the brake pedal, hoping I could stop before I broke through the gates. I left a short set of skid marks as my antilock brakes helped me stop straight without losing control. I banged my fist on the steering wheel and cursed under my breath as I watched those annoying red lights flash, alternating from left to right.

I could see the light from the train headed down the tracks. I thought for a moment that I might try going around the crossing gates, but it was difficult to judge the speed of the train. I watched the taillights of Ralph's car disappear on the horizon. The annoying bright lights of a vehicle reflected in my rearview mirror as it rolled up to my bumper. I adjusted my mirror to deflect the glare. I reached into my purse and rummaged for my cell phone. Now would be a good time to call Sam with the bad news. The Explorer jerked a little and felt as though it had been bumped from behind. I glanced in my mirror. I could no longer see the headlights of the car behind me. Not because it was gone, but because it was pushed right up against my bumper.

"Hey!" I shouted, as it continued to push my Explorer toward the red-and-white striped crossing gates. I shoved my foot down hard on the brake pedal. The crossing gates splintered and gave way to the grille of my Ford. My seat vibrated. I couldn't tell if it was from the friction of my locked wheels being shoved across the pavement, or the rumbling freight train barreling down the iron rails toward me. My eyes fixed on the bright strobe light headed in my direction. At that moment, I knew the fear of a deer, frozen in the headlights of a speeding truck as it stands in the center of the road, unable to move. A voice in my head said, *Think, Devonie! Think!* I snapped out of the trance, pushed the clutch to the floor, shoved the gearshift into first, and jammed my foot onto the gas pedal. Tires spun and smoke billowed from under the wheels as I crashed through the set of crossing gates on the other side of the tracks, just as the speeding train blasted through the intersection.

I stopped to recapture my breath. I cranked around in my seat and watched the rail cars speed past. The lights of the murderous vehicle flashed off and on as the gaps between the cars allowed the beams to pass through. I tried to judge the length of the train in the dark. I wanted to be long gone before the last car rolled through the intersection and allowed my attacker to resume the assault.

With a death grip on the wheel, I accelerated down the highway, the speedometer gauge pegged. I ran the events of the last twenty minutes over in my mind. Someone must have seen me at Ralph Campbell's house—someone who didn't want me following Ralph. Maybe Ralph had a partner in crime. Maybe Bradley Parker didn't want me to talk to Ralph.

I checked my rearview mirror. Lights from several cars were behind me. I made a turn and waited to see if any of them followed. They all continued on the main highway. I pulled to the shoulder of the road and cut the engine. The copies I'd made of Diane Parker's address book were sitting on the passenger seat next to me. I'd never taken them out of the Explorer. I powered on my cell phone and started calling every number. I asked to speak to the person from Diane's book, and once it was confirmed that person was home, I feigned phone trouble and disconnected the call. Then I crossed the name off the list and went on to the next. I didn't know who just tried to kill me, but I could start eliminating possibilities. When I finished, I'd only confirmed ten people were home and could not have been in the vicinity when I had my close encounter of the Southern Pacific kind. Bradley Parker wasn't one of them—he never picked up his phone.

I traversed the roadways and managed to make my way back to the city limits. As far as I could tell, no one followed me, but I still didn't want to go home. I drove to the police station and called Sam's house from my cell phone. He didn't answer, but I left a frantic message on his machine. I eyed the lights in the windows of the building I was parked in front of. I wondered if he could be working late tonight. I called his desk and was greeted by another recording. I blurted the highlights of my thrilling evening into his voice mailbox and begged him to return my call as soon as he got the message.

## Chapter Twelve

I slept like a mouse in a boa constrictor's cage. I woke up every hour, thinking I heard something or someone outside on the dock. I'd sit up and peer through the porthole, but not see anything. Then I'd worry and wonder why Sam hadn't returned my call. Was he punishing me for disobeying his orders? Maybe he'd finally had enough of me and shoved my Explorer in front of that train to get rid of me. *Now you're really being paranoid, Devonie,* I thought to myself.

When the sun finally peeked over the horizon, I decided it was useless to try for any more sleep. It wasn't going to happen. I dragged myself out of bed and into the galley. A note stuck to my refrigerator reminded me I was supposed to meet Pamela for lunch today. She wanted to update me on all she'd accomplished with her wedding plans.

I plucked a banana from my fruit bowl and peeled it as I booted up my computer. I logged into the eBay Web site to check the status of a bid I had on a rare, out-of-print video. I'd been trying to buy the video over the course of several weeks on three consecutive auctions, but someone managed to outbid me at the last minute every time. So far, I hadn't been outbid on this fourth auction, but that didn't mean anything. I didn't have my hopes up. While I was logged in, I decided to do a little snooping around. You never know what kind of bargain you might find on the Internet.

Pamela had actually made a lot of progress during the week. She'd hired a photographer, made arrangements with a florist, and mailed all the invitations. It looked like she was actually going to pull this wedding off, much to my dismay. I felt horrible, like animal control officers must feel when they deliver an innocent puppy to the pound. How could I continue to help her down the path to a condemned life with Bradley Parker, a confirmed anti-husband and possible murderer?

I took the last bite of my sandwich and pushed my plate away. "So did you go out with Bradley last night?" I asked.

She frowned. "We were supposed to go to the movies, but he called and canceled at the last minute. He had to go out of town for a couple days on business."

Out of town. I wonder if he took the train.

"Are you still thinking of buying a wedding gift for him?" I asked.

She nodded. "I'd like to, but I just don't know what to get him."

"I saw a credenza listed on eBay this morning. It matches the furniture in his office. You think he'd like something like that?"

Pamela's eyes lit up. "That's perfect. He'd love it."

I scratched my head and gave her a troubled look. "Only problem, it's pretty big. There might not be room. We'd have to take some measurements of his office," I said.

She smiled widely. "This is perfect. He's out of town. We can do it right now and he'll never know."

We stood in the center of Bradley Parker's office. I rummaged through my purse, feigning frustration. "I *always* carry a tape measure with me. I can't understand why it's not here."

Pamela peered into my purse, hoping she could spot it. She wouldn't, of course. The only tape measure I own is in my toolbox on the *Plan C*. Pamela inquired with the office staff. Luckily, no one had any sort of measuring device.

I dropped my shoulders in disappointment. "I'll just run home and get one. It should only take about twenty minutes," I offered.

"Nonsense. I'll run down to the hardware store. I'll be back in ten minutes, tops," Pamela insisted.

I smiled at her as if she'd just offered to donate a kidney. "Are you sure? It's really no problem."

"I insist," she said, halfway out the door. "I'll be right back."

She wasn't gone ten seconds before I was rummaging through Bradley's files. I wanted to find anything that showed he had a connection to SONGS. I rifled through his drawers, checked his Rolodex, and scanned his calendar. Nothing. I bumped his computer mouse and his monitor lit up. I rolled the chair up to the PC and searched his directories. His files were poorly named—giving no clue to what they contained. His directory structure was a mess, too. How could a computer professional be so disorganized and illogical? I tried an advanced search for any files containing the words "San Onofre" or "SONGS." I wasn't getting any hits.

I nervously checked my watch. Pamela would be back soon, and I didn't want her to catch me with my hand in the cookie jar. That's when I noticed the small, ball-shaped device sitting on Bradley's desk, next to his phone. I recognized it as a video camera, used for video conferencing. I'd also seen them used in conjunction with motion detectors for security purposes. I swallowed hard. If the device was recording, I could be in big trouble.

I heard Pamela's voice in the outer office. I hit the power button on the monitor and it went black.

She walked in just in time to catch me admiring a photo of her and Bradley getting ready to board a cruise ship. "Great picture," I commented, nodding toward the frame on Bradley's desk. "Where was it taken?"

"We took a three-day cruise to Mexico a couple of months ago. That's when he proposed," she replied, almost giddy.

Mexico. Memories of trips south of the border flashed through my mind. Over the years, I've compiled a list of things not to do in Mexico. Don't drink the water. Don't eat the food washed with the water. Don't drive your own car there. Don't ride in a taxi—which is very unhandy considering the previous entry in the list. I'd have to add another "don't" to my list. Do not accept proposals of marriage, especially from a man whose first wife died from a fall off a cliff.

We took measurements of the office and noted them down on a scratch pad. I nodded toward Bradley's computer. "He probably has Internet access. Let's log on to eBay and I'll show you the credenza. If you like it, we'll submit a bid and cross our fingers."

"Neat. You just find something you want and bid on it?"

"That's right. But don't assume it's a sure thing. I get outbid all the time," I explained. I powered the monitor on and clicked on the Internet Explorer icon. Pamela pulled a chair up next to me and watched the pages paint on the screen, like a gambler watching the wheels spin on a slot machine. I found the credenza and submitted Pamela's bid. I used my account, so all notifications would come to my e-mail address. That also meant that if the bid was successful, I was responsible for making sure the payment was made. If Pamela miraculously recovered from her severe case of love-blindness and called off the wedding, I could be stuck with the credenza. I decided it would be worth it and, in fact, almost hoped for it.

I arrived back at the *Plan C* and checked my answering machine. No messages. Why hadn't Sam called? Didn't he care that someone tried to kill me last night?

I'd struck out in Bradley's office. I couldn't find anything that connected him with SONGS. What was worse, I might have given myself away snooping in his files if that camera was on. I couldn't wait for Sam to call. I had to keep searching.

I dressed myself up in corporate attire once again and pranced up the dock in my navy-blue pumps, trying not to let the heels get caught between the planks. The new tires on my Explorer squealed a little as I rushed out of the marina parking lot.

San Onofre Nuclear Generating Station is situated ten

miles south of San Clemente. It sits right on the coast and is cooled by Pacific Ocean water. I pulled into the visitor center parking area and followed the directions the man in the guard shack gave me. I walked into the learning center building as if I belonged there and strolled up to the receptionist desk.

"Hi. I wonder if you can tell me the name of your IT manager?" I requested.

She smiled at me. "Certainly. His name is Wilbur Moore."

I made a note in the day planner I'd carried in with me. "I don't have an appointment, but I wonder if it would be possible to see him?" I requested.

She frowned at me. "He's not expecting you? He's very busy."

I flipped through pages in the planner and sighed. "Oh, I'm sure he must be, what with all the commotion about Ralph Campbell." I noticed the name on her employee badge. "Your name is Yvonne?" I asked, writing it down.

She eyed me suspiciously. "Yes. Ralph Campbell? Has something happened to Ralph?"

I stopped writing and gawked at her. "You mean you haven't heard?"

"All I know is he didn't show up for work today. No one has been able to get in touch with him or his wife. Is he okay?" she asked, concerned.

I closed the planner and slipped it under my arm. "I'd better not say any more until I've spoken with Mr. Moore. Can you tell him that Lillian Schockley is here to see him?"

Yvonne punched some keys on her switchboard and greeted Wilbur Moore. "Wilbur? There's a Lillian Schockley here to see you. She has information about Ralph Campbell."

I smiled as I listened to her end of the conversation.

"I don't know," she whispered into the headset. "She didn't tell me. She'll only talk to you," she explained. "Okay. I'll have Donna bring her to your office."

Wilbur Moore stood when I entered his office and reached out to shake my hand. "I'm Wilbur Moore. And you're Lillian . . . ?" He checked a note he'd written on his desk.

"Schockley. Lillian Schockley," I said, gripping his hand and nearly shaking his arm out of its socket. "Thank you so much for seeing me."

Wilbur was a short, stocky man. His wiry hair formed clumps of curly gray over each ear. The top of his head was smooth and shiny and reminded me of one of the two containment domes I'd seen outside, used to house the re-actor vessels and steam generators. At least that's what Donna told me they were, as she gave me a very brief plant tour on our way to Wilbur's office. He'd developed the typical potbelly so common among men his age who sit behind a desk all day.

"You have information about Ralph Campbell?" he asked, anxious to hear what I had to say.

"You haven't heard?" I replied, sounding astonished that word hadn't gotten around yet.

"No. What?"

I leaned forward in my chair and spoke quietly, as if the walls might have ears. "Bradley Parker hasn't contacted you?"

He gave me a confused look. "Bradley Parker?"

"About the lawsuit?" I added.

"Lawsuit?" He was in the dark.

I opened my day planner and flipped through pages. "You do run a software package called Voltage, don't you?" I asked, skimming pages of unrelated notes about sailboat maintenance schedules and caterer's menus.

"Yes. But what does that have to do with Ralph?" he asked, nervously pulling at the bushy eyebrow hairs over his left eye.

I clicked for more lead from my mechanical pencil and started scribbling. "You did purchase the Voltage package from Business Solutions, didn't you?" I said, more of a statement than a question.

"Business Solutions? Is that a local company?" he asked.

I stopped writing. "How long have you worked here?" I asked.

"Five years. But what does that have to do with—"

"So you didn't buy Voltage from Bradley Parker's company?" I interrupted.

"We purchased it directly from the vendor." Wilbur's voice raised an octave, and his frustration showed. "Who are you? What's happened to Ralph?" he demanded.

I slipped my pencil back in its slot and closed the planner. "I'm investigating the death of a friend. My search led me to Ralph Campbell. Did he tell you about a problem with the Voltage software? Something about a rounding error with the inventory balances?"

Wheels began turning inside Wilbur's head. I could see him trying to piece together events from the past. "Rounding? Gosh. That's been a couple years ago," he recalled.

"And you resolved it?" I asked.

"I told Ralph to take care of it. I'd assumed he did."

"So you're not involved in a lawsuit with the Voltage vendor?" I asked.

"Of course not," he insisted.

I leaned back in my chair and crossed my legs. "You are aware that the Voltage inventory module loses as much as a quarter pound per transaction due to a rounding bug?"

Wilbur gaped at me. He didn't speak.

"Ralph Campbell tried to explain this to you. Remember?" I added.

Wilbur nodded dumbly. "Where's Ralph?" he managed to ask.

I stood up. "I think I'd better let the police handle that discussion. I'm surprised they haven't already contacted you."

"Police?" he mumbled.

"You might want to contact your legal department." I reached for the door, stopped, and turned. "Do you have a lawyer, Mr. Moore?"

His pale face nodded. "We have a whole team of lawyers."

I gave him a worried look. "I don't mean SONGS. I mean you."

The expression on his sweaty face reminded me of someone who was about to be sick. I closed the door behind me and headed for the exit. I had a feeling things would be heating up soon at San Onofre Nuclear Generating Station, and it wasn't going to be from a nuclear reaction.


Sam was waiting on the dock next to the *Plan C* when I arrived home. I approached him cautiously, wondering if I was in big trouble.

"You okay?" he asked.

I nodded. "Fine. You got my message?"

"I did." He nodded toward the sixty-foot sailboat tied in the slip. "Nice boat."

"Thanks." I stepped over the railing. "Come on in. I'll show you around."

He followed me into the main salon. I noticed the message light flashing on my answering machine. He noticed, too.

"Probably my messages. I've been trying to reach you all afternoon."

"Did you come up with anything? Got any ideas who tried to kill me last night?" I asked.

"No. You have a description of the vehicle?"

"It was dark. All I could see were headlights," I explained.

He frowned at me. "What were you doing out there?"

"You know what I was doing. I told you in my message. Ralph Campbell was on the run, and I was following him. Whoever it was didn't want me to catch up with him. It's probably Ralph's partner in crime," I speculated.

"Better try another theory," he said.

I walked into the galley and opened the refrigerator. "Want something to drink? I've got iced tea, juice, water. . . ." I offered.

"Iced tea. Thanks," he replied.

I poured two glasses and handed him one. "What do you mean 'another theory?' " I asked.

Sam took a long drink of tea, then set the glass on a coaster. "I got called out late last night."

I stared at him, waiting for more. "And . . . ?"

"Ralph Campbell's dead. Murdered."

## Chapter Thirteen

The car Ralph Campbell was driving was found wrapped around the trunk of an old oak tree. His body was nearly inseparable from the mangled frame of the Volvo. There were no witnesses to the accident, and I wondered how Sam could be sure it wasn't more than just that—an accident. Ralph was in a panic. Maybe he took the turn too fast and lost control. Maybe he thought about a life on the run, or worse, in prison and decided to end it all. I ran those possibilities by Sam. He shook his head.

"Coroner owed me a favor. He put a rush on Campbell's autopsy," Sam explained.

"And . . . ?"

"Campbell was dead before he ever hit the tree. Had a bullet in his brain. Forty-five caliber. Entered the skull just behind his left ear."

I shivered at the thought. "Guess a seat belt wouldn't have made a difference, then," I said.

Sam shook his head again. "So, whoever tried to get you

out of the picture may have been on Ralph's tail to begin with. He probably didn't want an audience."

I closed my eyes and tried to remember every detail from the night before. Had I seen any other cars parked in front of Campbell's house? I couldn't recall anything. I was doing the following, so I wasn't expecting to be followed myself. I snapped my fingers and opened my eyes, searching for my purse.

"After my near train disaster, I called all the numbers in Diane's phone book to see who wasn't home at the time," I said as I crossed the salon and pulled the folded copy of Diane's phone book from my purse. I handed it to Sam and pointed out the crossed out names.

"Those people were home, so I figure they're off the suspect list," I explained.

Sam studied the copies. "What are you doing with this?"

"I copied Diane's phone book before I gave it to you," I admitted.

"Why?" he questioned.

I didn't say a word, but gave him a look that said exactly what I was thinking.

"Stupid question," he replied, reading my mind.

I pointed to the book again. "Bradley Parker wasn't home. He had to leave on an unplanned business trip, according to his fiancée."

"So you're still set on making Bradley Parker a murderer?" Sam asked.

"Well, now I'm not so sure. He didn't sell the Voltage software to SONGS, so our theory that he killed Diane to protect his business from another lawsuit kind of fizzles," I explained.

"*Our* theory?"

I ignored his comment. "So if Bradley didn't do it, who did?"

Sam paged through the copies in his hand. "None of these people are suspects. My guess is Campbell had a connection in the plutonium trade. Whoever that is didn't want him saying any more than he already had."

"So you think Campbell told his story to Diane, and that's why she's dead?" I asked.

"Possibly."

"But how did Ralph survive so long? Wouldn't he have been killed at the same time? It doesn't make sense," I argued.

"Ralph survived because he sold his soul to the devil. He took their money and got caught up in the consequences of his greed. The deeper he got in, the more he had to lose if he spilled his guts."

Garrett Henderson seemed genuinely pleased to see me. "Devonie. What a nice surprise. Any luck on your investigation?" he asked.

I followed him into his office and took a seat across from his desk. "Not really," I replied. The ringing phones and general noise from the hustle and bustle of the newspaper business was muted when he closed his door.

"Too bad. I was hoping we could report Bradley Parker had been arrested for the brutal murder of his wife," Garrett mused.

"Actually, it's looking like maybe he's not the culprit, after all," I said.

Garrett seemed surprised. "Really? What brings you to that conclusion?"

I'd asked myself that same question over and over as I

drove to the *Union Tribune* building. I couldn't connect
Bradley Parker to the plutonium missing from SONGS, but
did that mean he wasn't guilty? Before I'd discovered the
Ralph Campbell connection, I was sure Parker killed Diane
out of pure meanness. Maybe the fact that Diane had the
"Science Project" video in her belongings was pure coincidence.

"There've been new developments," I offered. "It's sort
of complicated. It would be really helpful if I could find
out exactly what Diane was working on when she died."

Garrett frowned and scratched his head. "That's a tough
one." He glanced around the piles of papers and notebooks
on his desk. He shoved some folders aside and pulled a
leather binder from under a stack of black-and-white pho-
tographs. He opened it up flat on his desk and paged
through the calendar section. "I'll check my notes from last
year," he said, licking his thumb and turning the pages. He
ran his finger down each page, searching for some specific
entry. "Ah. Here. I have a note that Diane would cover the
annual Kennel Club dog show. That was the week before
she died." He continued flipping pages. "She covered a
fashion show, interviewed teachers and school board mem-
bers—"

"What school?" I interrupted.

Garrett adjusted the glasses on his nose and studied his
notes. "It doesn't appear I wrote it down."

"Could it have been Lincoln High?" I asked, hopeful.

Garrett searched his memory. He closed his eyes and
turned his face toward the ceiling. "Lincoln, Lincoln," he
repeated. "No, I don't think it was Lincoln. It was an elementary school. Ten-year-olds selling drugs to other ten-
year-olds. Believe that? Now I remember. Terrible story."

I gawked at him. "Ten-year-old drug dealers?"

"And users. Sorry society we're living in," he replied.

I shook my head, dismayed. "How about something she might have been working on off the record? You know, a career-promoting story? A personal project?"

Garrett nodded. "She was a go-getter. Wouldn't surprise me to find out she was pounding the pavement to dig up her own story." He pushed his chair away from his desk and slid open a file drawer. "I copied her electronic files from her computer before we let her replacement use it. Anything she was working on for the paper would have been saved to the main server, but if she was working on something on her own, she probably would have kept it on her own machine until she was ready to show it to me."

He removed a box of computer disks from the drawer and flipped through them. "Here we are," he said, pulling one labeled *Diane Parker Files* out of the stack. He slid it into his disk drive and brought up the list of files contained on the disk. We both read down the short list of files in a folder called *Notes*.

"Highland Elementary," Garrett read aloud. "That's the school story. Let's see. Kennel Club. That's the fashion show," he kidded. "I mean, dog show," he continued, chuckling.

His humor evaded me. I was concentrating on the last file in the list. "What's this one?" I asked, pointing at the screen. "Spousal abuse."

Garrett hovered the mouse pointer over the file. "I don't know. Let's take a look," he said, opening the document.

The double-spaced manuscript painted itself on the screen and we both read the first few paragraphs in silence.

*Realizing Your Value*
*by Diane Parker*

*Do you ever wonder why you were put on this
Earth? Do you ever think maybe you're here by mistake? I asked myself those very questions every day
for nearly twenty years.*

*When I was a young girl, I couldn't hear—or re-
fused to listen to—people who told me how pretty I
was, or how smart I was, or how talented I was. I
thought,* They're just saying that, but they don't really
mean it. *Why couldn't I believe them? They were my
family, my parents, my close friends, my teachers.
Why would they lie?*

*Instead, I chose to believe the mean, hateful things
that young people tend to say to other young people.
People who don't even know you. People who say
things like, "You're ugly. You're stupid. You're
clumsy. You're worthless." People who cannot feel
good about themselves without making others feel
bad. People who feel they've raised themselves up a
notch by knocking everyone else down.*

Diane's manuscript went on for pages and made it clear
that her soon-to-be ex-husband was one of those people
who raised himself up by knocking others down. Garrett
and I read it completely. I wanted to cry by the time I
reached the end. I wanted to grab Bradley Parker by the
throat and squeeze until his face turned blue. I wanted to
strip him of all his arrogance and parade him, naked, in
front of the whole world and let it see his ugliness.

Garrett leaned back in his chair and ran his fingers

through his hair. "Wow. This is good. I wish she had let me see it when she wrote it." He thought for a moment. "I might run it anyway. I think I'll save it out on the server and have someone polish it up." He clicked the "Save As" menu selection and saved a copy of the file to some remote computer in some distant room or building. Then he ejected the disk.

"Can I have that?" I asked.

Garrett studied it momentarily. "Sure. I saved what I wanted. Maybe you can get something out of it that will help nail the guy." He handed me the disk. "You know, Parker had a big insurance policy on Diane. She was definitely worth more to him dead than alive."

So here I was, back at square one. I'd made a full circle. Maybe my first instinct was right. Bradley Parker killed his wife for the insurance money. He loved his business more than he loved her. Somehow, I had to prove it.

My phone was ringing when I entered the *Plan C*. I managed to pick it up before the answering machine did. "Hello?"

"Devonie. Oh, it's awful. I can't believe it. It's off. The whole thing is off," the voice sobbed.

"Pamela?" I asked.

"Yes. I don't know what to do. I feel so stupid. How could I have been so—"

"What's wrong, Pamela? Tell me what happened," I cut in.

"It's Bradley. How could he be so cruel? So cold. Did he think I had an unbreakable heart?" She sobbed into the phone.

Sympathetic tears welled up in my eyes. "Where are you? At your apartment?" I asked.

Her voice quivered. "Y-yes, but—"

"I'll be right there. You can have dinner with Craig and me."

"I don't want to talk about it. It's too painful," she said.

"Fine. We won't talk about it. We'll rent a movie. We'll play cards. We'll bake cookies. We'll take your mind off it. You shouldn't be alone right now. I'll be there in twenty minutes. Okay?"

Her response was barely audible. "Okay," she whispered, her voice cracking.

I called Craig to warn him I was bringing an emotional female over for some serious mind-distraction therapy for a broken heart.

"Should I get my medical bag?" he asked.

"Not necessary," I assured him. "But could you pick up a movie? No romantic comedies. No love stories."

"Okay. How about action adventure?" he suggested.

"Perfect. And could you find some playing cards or some games?" I asked.

"Sure. Anything else?"

I thought for a moment. "Chocolate. Lots of chocolate."

"Got it. I'll get the supplies, you get the patient. I'll see you here in forty-five minutes."

"Thanks, Craig. You're an angel," I told him.

"I do have to admit, I am the pick of the litter."

I smiled at his comment. He was better than the pick of the litter. In my book, he was best in show.


I rang the bell at Pamela's apartment. There was no answer. I held my ear to the door and rang it again. Yes, it was working. I could hear it ring inside. She was probably trying to get her face to look like she hadn't been crying for hours. I waited. I rang again. I knocked. "Pamela?" I called. "Are you there?" No response. I banged on the door. "Pamela!"

I made such a ruckus, the neighbor in the apartment next door poked his head out. "She's not home," he said, irritated.

"I just spoke to her on the phone. I was supposed to pick her up. I think she may be in trouble in there," I explained.

"She's not in trouble. She left five minutes ago. I saw her leave," he insisted.

"You're sure she left?" I asked.

He rolled his eyes. "She left. Okay? Got in that fancy car of her boyfriend's and they drove off."

"Her boyfriend? You mean Bradley?" I asked.

"Yeah. That's his name. They took off. Like I said, five minutes ago. So quit bangin'. I'm trying to watch the game."

I gawked at the beer-bellied, unshaven man standing in his doorway, wearing Bermuda shorts and a faded T-shirt. He stepped back and started to push the door closed. I shoved my hand out and held it firm against the door, preventing him from closing it.

"Wait. Did she look like she . . . was she . . . did she want to go with him?" I asked.

He gaped at me as though my question were as ridiculous as asking a fourteen-year-old boy if he'd rather be a professional baseball player or a garbage collector. "Did she *want* to go with him? Are you kidding? The guy drives a Mercedes. What do you think?"

I smirked. "Of course. The Mercedes. If Charles Manson

had only driven a Mercedes, I'm sure his trial would have had a completely different outcome. And just think how Attila the Hun could have changed his image if only Mercedes made a chariot."

He held his hands out and waved them in self-defense. "I just meant that—"

"I know what you meant. All women are gold diggers who value money over kindness and character," I interrupted.

"I didn't say that. Look, I just want to watch my game," he insisted, trying to force the door closed.

"Can you just tell me if she looked happy to be going with him?" I asked.

He scratched the round belly hanging out from the hem of his overstretched T-shirt. "She was crying, but that don't mean nothin'. Women cry all the time."

I nodded with acknowledgment. *If his perception is that women cry all the time, then it must be his effect on them that has made this his reality,* I thought to myself.

I removed my hand from his door and he slammed it shut. "Prince Charming," I muttered to myself as I raced down the stairs and back to the Explorer. I jumped inside, started the engine, then sat there. Where would I go? What could I do? I banged my fists on the steering wheel in frustration. Bradley had hooked her and was reeling her in.

## Chapter Fourteen

"Can't you put out an APB or something?" I demanded, grasping the edge of Sam's desk as I stood over him, trying to assume an intimidating stance.

"I could, if some crime had been committed," Sam replied, through gritted teeth.

"Crime! I think he's kidnapped her! That's a crime," I argued.

"You have a witness?" he asked.

"Yes. Her neighbor. He told me she was crying when she left with Bradley."

"Was she screaming and kicking? Biting? Punching? Fighting? Anything that might suggest she was being taken against her will?"

"No. But—"

"But nothing. If I arrested every guy who made his wife or girlfriend cry, the entire male population would be behind bars," Sam insisted as he stood up and towered over me.

I stood my ground and raised my chin so I could look him square in the eye. "What if Bradley did kill Diane? Pamela could be in trouble. You have to do something."

"What do you want me to do? We checked her apartment. No sign of trouble. We sent a patrol car by his house. No one there. He's not at his office. There's nothing to do but wait," he insisted.

"Wait for what? Pamela's body to wash up on the beach?"

I checked the paper for information on Ralph Campbell's funeral. Graveside services would be held at a local cemetery. Afterward, friends could express their condolences to the family at the home of the widow's sister. I noted the address and checked the time.

I sat in my Explorer parked in front of the house and watched the mourners, dressed in black, make their way to the front door. I recognized some of the visitors as SONGS employees, whom I'd seen on my visit there.

I brushed some lint off of my black skirt and slipped out of the car. A couple walked down the sidewalk, each carrying a foil-covered dish. I suddenly felt unprepared. Was I supposed to bring food? I was reminded how lucky I was that I'd never had to attend a gathering like this before. The couple regarded me with somber nods as I crossed the street. I fell into step behind the pair and followed them into the house.

I felt a little guilty because I wasn't really here to pay my respects, but to dig up information. If I couldn't connect Bradley Parker to SONGS, maybe I could connect him to Ralph Campbell.

Hilary Campbell sat perched on the edge of the sofa.

Sympathetic guests surrounded her, trying to offer comfort and support. I meekly approached her and offered my hand. "I'm so sorry, Mrs. Campbell," I said.

She looked at me and forced a teary smile. Her expression was a little confused. "Thank you. Do I know you?"

"No. I knew Ralph from SONGS," I told her.

"Oh," she replied, then wiped her eyes with a tissue.

I backed away to allow others—more appropriate comfort-givers—access to the sorrowful woman. I headed for the kitchen where a young man was offering glasses of water and sodas. A heavy-set Hispanic woman was pulling tamales out of a huge pot of boiling water on the stove and placing them on a large platter. Dishes of every kind of food imaginable covered the counters. There was barely room to set anything down.

"Do you have lemon?" I asked, as the boy handed me a glass of water.

"Right there," he said, pointing to a bowl of lemon wedges, sitting next to a pitcher of iced tea.

I squeezed the lemon in my water and headed back toward the living room. The woman at the stove stopped her scooping and turned to face me. "You from Ralph's work?" she asked, wiping her hands on her apron.

"I knew him from SONGS. Yes," I replied.

She squinted at me. "I'm Maria. I work for the Campbells. I never see you before."

"We weren't close."

"Ralph was a very friendly man. Invited all his friends from work for parties. I cook. You never came?"

I shook my head. "Like I said, we weren't close."

She nodded. "Hmm. Then why are you here now?"

I set my glass on the one small square of free space on

the counter. I stared at the ceiling for a moment to gather my thoughts, then looked back into the woman's dark eyes. "Because something inside me told me it was the right thing to do."

She studied my face, then shoved the platter of tamales at me. "You're a good girl. Have a tamale. Very good. I make them myself. You'll like it."

I smiled and found a paper plate. I took one tamale. She forced a second one on my plate. "You're too skinny. Need more than one. Here."

"Thank you. So, you're the Campbells' housekeeper?" I asked.

She smiled proudly. "Yes. Two years. Very nice family."

I took a bite of the tamale. "Mmm. Very good," I said, wiping my mouth. "Then you must know Bradley Parker?"

She searched her memory. "Bradley Parker?"

"Yes. I think he was a business associate of Mr. Campbell's—tall, light hair, slender," I said, hoping to spark a memory.

She shook her head. "I don't know. Many friends came. I don't know all their names."

I nodded with understanding.

She returned to her cooking, and I headed toward a group of mourners gathered around a bowl of chips and salsa. I recognized one of them from my brief visit to SONGS. A hungry-looking man with a mouthful of corn chips eyed my plate of tamales.

"Where'd you get that?" he asked, almost drooling.

I pointed toward the kitchen, and he was gone before I could get a word out.

"You'll have to excuse Ruben. He skipped breakfast. He

swears he has a blood-sugar problem," a young woman from the group explained.

I smiled and picked up a scoop of salsa with a chip. "I thought I saw Bradley Parker at the funeral. Have any of you seen him here?" I asked.

They exchanged glances, then looked back at me with frowns. "Don't know who he is," they said, almost in unison.

I wandered from guest to guest, casually mentioning Parker's name and hoping for a response. No one knew who he was. I began to doubt my theory that Parker and Campbell had a connection. I plopped down on the couch and watched poor little Mike play with a small toy Corvette—red, like his dad's. He pushed it around on the floor, but with little enthusiasm.

The woman from the couple I'd seen when I first arrived approached and sat next to me on the couch. She had a plate of chocolate-chip cookies.

"Cookie?" she offered.

I took one from the plate, then she set it on the coffee table. "Thank you," I said.

"I just can't believe this has happened," she blurted.

"I know. It's terrible," I replied.

"Poor little Mike. Just look at him over there. Can you imaging losing your dad at his age?"

I shook my head. "No. It's going to be hard for him, I'm sure."

The woman picked up a cookie and took a bite. "Did you work with Ralph?" she asked, chewing the cookie between words.

"Sort of," I answered.

"I thought so. But I hadn't seen you at the house for a while. I thought maybe you got a new car," she said.

I looked at her, confused. "New car?"

"Yeah. The orange one? I used to see it parked out front some nights, but that's been at least a year. Figured you got a new one or something," she explained.

I had a sudden hope that this busybody neighbor knew more about what was happening in her neighborhood than anyone else. "I didn't buy a new one, but I took on a new position about a year ago, and my schedule changed. I couldn't come over like I used to, you know."

"I can understand that. Gee. Seems like you were there every Wednesday evening, then poof, you quit coming," she said.

I smiled and nodded. "Yeah. The new position meant a lot more responsibility and late hours at the office. I barely had time to pet my cat, let alone visit friends."

She seemed satisfied with my story. She picked up the plate of cookies and stood up. "I better see if anyone else wants a cookie before I eat the whole batch."

I stopped her briefly and took another cookie from the plate. She wandered off to another corner and peddled her goodies to other guests.

I wrapped the cookie in a napkin and walked across the room to little Mike, sitting cross-legged on the floor with his toy car. I kneeled down and handed him the cookie. "Here. Thought you might want it for later," I offered.

He took it and set it in his lap. "I remember you. You have a funny name."

"That's right. Devonie. How ya doin'?"

"Okay, I guess," he said, staring down at his hands. "This

is my car," he continued, holding up the small replica of his father's Corvette.

"It's cool," I said, admiring it.

"It's just like my dad's," he boasted.

"I know."

"My dad's not here. He had to go away," he explained.

"I know."

"I don't know when he's coming back," he said.

I put my hand on his little shoulder. "I don't know, either."

I stopped in the kitchen on the way out and thanked Maria for the tamales. She pushed a foil-covered plate full of a dozen more into my hands and sent me on my way. "Too skinny. You eat."

I slid into the driver's seat and retrieved the cell phone from my purse. I punched in Sam's number and listened to his recording.

"Sam. It's Devonie. You're not gonna believe it. Looks like we need to take a closer look at Willy Mendenhal. I'll fill you in later. Call me when you get this."

## Chapter Fifteen

Willy Mendenhal's shifty little eyes darted quickly from Sam's stern face to mine, then back to Sam's.

"I'm tellin' you, I don't know no Ralph Campbell. You got the wrong guy," Willy insisted.

"I don't think so. I talked to some people who said they saw your car parked in front of Ralph's house almost every Wednesday night before you checked into this prison," I replied.

Willy's face turned into a collection of creases and drops of sweat. "That's bull," he finally whined. "I ain't never been near the guy's house."

"Thought you said you didn't know him," Sam said.

"I don't."

"Then how do you know you've never been near his house?" Sam pressed.

Willy's whining grew more intense. "This is harassment—pure and simple. I got rights. You can't just come in here and accuse me without any proof."

I waited for Sam's rebuttal, but there wasn't one. I decided to take the conversation in a new direction. "So, what's the going rate for plutonium these days, Willy?"

His face turned pale and his chin dropped. "Plu . . . plutonium? Hey, man. I for sure don't know nothin' about no plutonium. You're diggin' up the wrong weed."

Sam leaned forward in his chair, his face only inches from Willy's. I took note of his clenched jaw, the tension barometer I'd learned to read, and was thankful I wasn't on the receiving end of his anger. "Oh, I'm digging up the right weed, all right," he hissed. "I'm gonna keep digging. When I find out you and Campbell were in the plutonium business, and you killed Diane Parker, you're coming up by the roots. You got that?"

Willy looked at me with pleading eyes. Tears started rolling down his face. "I swear I didn't have nothin' to do with that lady. I just took her stuff. That's all. And I don't know nothin' about no plutonium. You gotta believe me."

I didn't respond. If Willy ever had any credibility, he'd done a good job of destroying it. He certainly hadn't done anything to earn my faith in his words. He directed his pleading eyes at Sam.

Sam shoved his chair back and stood up. He pointed his finger in Willy's face. "By the roots."

I followed Sam out to his car. "You think he's lying?" I asked, trying to keep up with his frenetic pace.

"Could be. But he's right. Without proof, we can't do a thing to him. He'll be out on the street in six months unless we can connect him with Campbell."

I jogged a few steps to catch up. "What about the neighbor who saw the car in front of Ralph's house?"

"Can't prove it was the same car without the license

number. As hard as I find it to believe, Ford put that color on more than one Explorer. Could have been someone else's car parked there. We need something more solid."

I slid into the passenger seat and slammed the door shut. Sam stared out the windshield for a few seconds, then started the engine and backed out of the parking space.

Sam dropped me off at the marina and headed back to the station. He said he had work piling up around his ears and couldn't afford to spend all his time on this one case. When I offered to take on more investigative duties, he laughed and drove away. I shook my fist at his taillights and headed for my mailbox.

I tossed my purse on the sofa and flipped through the stack of mail. Junk. Junk. Junk. *Wait a minute. What's this?* I inspected the envelope closely, front and back. I tore it open and pulled the contents out. "What?" I complained. It was a traffic citation—complete with a photo of my Explorer and me at the wheel, apparently exceeding the speed limit. "You've got to be kidding," I whined.

I read through all the fine print and concluded that I would indeed be paying the fine and attending the next available traffic school session to keep the whole ugly incident off my driving record. I stuffed the documents back in the envelope and filed it away to be dealt with later.

There was still a dark cloud looming overhead—Pamela's disappearance. I'd called her apartment a dozen times, but got no answer. I called Craig to see if he'd heard from her. Not a word.

Something didn't feel right. If Willy Mendenhal was responsible for Diane Parker's death, or even involved, then where did that leave Bradley Parker as a suspect? Could he have a connection to Willy that I hadn't uncovered yet? At any rate, I couldn't stop worrying about Pamela. I gathered up my purse and keys and headed for the marina parking lot.

It was a gorgeous day in La Jolla. The sun shone brightly on the sparkling blue Pacific as I eased my way north toward Bradley Parker's house. I pulled into his driveway and admired the view for a moment before I marched to his front door, ready to attack him if he gave even the slightest hint that he'd hurt Pamela.

Parker answered the door, still in his robe. I could smell brandy on his breath. "Pamela's not here," he grumbled, before I'd even asked.

"Do you—"

He closed the door before I could get the question out. Irritated, I rang the bell, again.

He reappeared, his bloodshot eyes squinting at me as though I were a lowly creature, unworthy of his precious time. "I told you, she's not here."

"I know. Do you know where she is?" I asked, trying to keep my cool.

"Not exactly, no," he slurred. He'd had more to drink than I'd first realized. He started to close the door again, but this time I put my hand out and stopped him.

"Wait. You saw her last, according to her neighbor. Where did you take her?"

He glared at me. "None of your business. Now get out of here and leave me alone."

I kept my arm braced firmly against the door he was still trying to close in my face. "No! You've done something to her, just like you did your wife! Tell me where she is or I'll—"

"My wife? You're crazy."

"I'm perfectly sane, Mr. Parker. You're the only one who had a motive to kill your wife—the divorce, the financial troubles with your business, the insurance money."

Parker's mouth hung half open. He swayed back and forth in the doorway, apparently dizzy from his drunkenness. "I didn't kill my wife," he hissed.

I returned his scowl. "Just like you haven't done anything to Pamela?"

He closed his eyes and rubbed his forehead with a trembling hand. "I dropped Pamela off at the airport yesterday. She got on the plane and flew away. I didn't do anything to her," he moaned. I couldn't tell if the pain in his voice came from the brandy or the loss of Pamela.

"Flew away? Where to?" I asked.

He shook his head. "I don't . . . Florida . . . yeah, Florida."

I eyed him suspiciously. It seemed to me he was just making up a story to pacify me. "Why Florida?"

He continued to massage his head, as though a great pounding was going on inside it. "I don't know. I think she said something about her mother. No, maybe it was her aunt. I think that's it."

"Her aunt? Was she ill or something?" I asked.

Parker aimed his red eyes at mine. "No. She wasn't ill. Pamela left me, and has gone to stay in Florida for good. Are you happy?"

*Elated,* I thought to myself. The poor girl finally wised up and opened her eyes. "Do you have a phone number or an address for her?"

He shook his head. "No. She didn't want to hear from me."

I removed my hand from the door. "What in the world did you do to her?" I asked, my voice shaking.

He stared at me for a long moment, then without saying a word, he closed the door.


Pamela staying with her aunt? I played the conversation with Bradley Parker over and over in my mind as I drove home. There was something wrong with his story. Pamela told me her parents were dead, and I remember her saying that Bradley was all the family she had. Wouldn't she consider an aunt family?

By the time I reached the marina, I'd convinced myself he was lying. I dialed Sam's number and waited for his answer.

"Sam Wright," he blurted into the phone.

"Devonie Lace," I blurted back.

"You again?" he whined. "I thought I'd get at least twenty-four hours before you'd start pestering me."

I ignored this. "Listen. I just got back from talking to Bradley Parker. He told me he put Pamela on a plane yesterday. Said she went to Florida to stay with her aunt."

"Good. Then we can stop worrying about her," he replied.

"I don't think so. As far as I know, she doesn't have an aunt. I think he's lying," I said.

"Do you know for sure?"

"Do I know anything for sure? She told me Bradley was all the family she had. Isn't it enough for you to at least question him?" I pleaded.

"Maybe. I'll look into it," he answered.

He'd look into it. I guess I'd have to be satisfied with that. It was better than a definite no, which is what I expected. "Hey, you wouldn't by any chance be able to pull some strings and take care of a traffic violation, could you?" I asked, fully expecting a ten-minute lecture on the importance of obeying all traffic laws.

"You got a ticket?" he asked.

"Yeah. One of those cameras took my picture. I was only going twelve miles over the limit. Got it in the mail today."

"Tough break. Guess you better slow down," he said.

"Guess so. Don't know if I like all this new technology. Seems like they could use it to catch the real criminals," I complained.

Sam didn't respond.

"You still there?" I asked.

"Yeah. I'm here. You just gave me an idea."

"I did? It doesn't involve me wearing stripes and living behind bars, does it?"

"No. No. Nothing like that. Listen. The picture on your citation—is it clear? Can you make out the license plate?" he asked.

I retrieved the envelope from where I'd filed it and pulled the photo out. "Yeah, clear as a bell. Why?"

"I don't know. It's just a hunch, and a long shot at that. You still set on helping me with this investigation?"

I almost fell out of my chair. "Are you asking me for help?"

"It won't be exciting. In fact, it'll probably put you to sleep, it'll be so tedious, but better you than me," he admitted.

"Gee. Thanks."

"Meet me down here at the station in an hour. I'll have to set it up first."

"Set what up?" I asked.

"You'll see when you get here."

Before I even had a chance to sit down in Sam's office, he took me by the arm and escorted me to another room. Inside, a man was busy sorting through a box of videotapes.

"Jay. This is Devonie Lace, the girl I told you about," Sam said.

The man looked up from his box of videos and smiled. "Nice to meet you," he said, holding out his hand.

"Jay's a big-shot down at Caltrans. He may be able to help us out with our Willy Mendenhal problem," Sam explained.

I was still at a loss. "How?" I questioned.

Jay pushed the box of videos aside and sat on the edge of the desk. "Caltrans uses video surveillance technology to study traffic patterns in certain areas that may require modifications," he explained.

"Modifications?" I asked.

"Yeah. You know. Overcrowding, gridlock, traffic jams," he continued.

"You must have cameras all over San Diego," I replied.

Jay chuckled. "Not yet, but you'd be surprised how many times your smiling face passes one of our lenses."

Sam pulled a videocassette from the box. "There are only two routes into the subdivision where Ralph Campbell's house is. Those routes are monitored by Caltrans. By some stroke of luck, the tapes from last year haven't been recorded over."

I peered into the box. There were dozens of videos.

"Jay pulled all the tapes for that area for every Wednesday between noon and eight."

My gaze met Sam's. "You think Willy and the Explorer are on these tapes?"

"Don't know. That's your job to find out," he replied.

Jay hoisted himself off the desk. "That's my cue to vamoose. You start watching those videos and the next thing you know, you're collapsed on the floor, your eyes closed and your mouth open."

Sam walked Jay to the door. "Thanks, buddy. What time does tomorrow's game start?" Sam asked.

"Eight," Jay answered.

"Great. See you then," Sam said as he let Jay through the door, closing it behind him.

"Game?" I asked.

"Poker. Every Thursday night."

"Gambling? You? Is that legal?" I asked, joking.

"Never mind. You better get busy," Sam said as he loaded a video into the VCR and pressed the PLAY button. "I'll check on you in a while to see how you're doing."

"You mean to see if I'm still awake?"

"That, too."

I glanced at the TV screen and my heart sank. "Wait a minute," I called to Sam before he could escape. "This is in black-and-white," I said.

"What did you expect? Technicolor?"

I sneered at him. "How am I supposed to spot an orange Explorer on this?"

Sam picked up the VCR remote and held it out to me. "When you see something that looks like an Explorer, pause it and check the license plate."

"You're kidding, right?"

"I thought you wanted to help. This is what I need you to do."

I snatched the remote from him and turned my attention back to the TV screen.

Sam paused in the doorway. "Don't be mad. It's time you learned that police work isn't all guns, glory, and excitement like in the movies." Then he was gone, and there I was with a box of tapes, a VCR, a TV, a remote, and nothing but time.

After five hours of watching car after car pass through the same intersections, I was convinced this was Sam's way to finally punish me for interfering with his work. Each time he poked his head through the door, my eyes were glazed over and I was trying a new and different position in the chair to try to keep alert—or at least awake.

In an act of mercy, Sam brought me a chocolate bar and a Coke. "Caffeine. Help keep you awake. After this, I have some paint drying in the other room I want you to watch."

"Very funny," I groaned.

By ten o'clock, I'd taken as much torture as I could. Sam finally returned to release me from my agony. "No luck, huh?"

I rubbed my tired eyes and moaned. "I checked every single SUV that passed through those intersections. Quite a few were regulars—same car, same time, every day, but none of them were mine."

Sam helped me to my feet. "Guess that lets Willy off the hook. Must have been a different vehicle the neighbor saw," he concluded.

"So, where does that leave us?" I asked.

"Back at the beginning."

"In other words—nowhere," I grumbled.

"Not exactly. We're going to pick up Bradley Parker tomorrow."

My eyes lit up. "You are?"

"Don't get excited. We're just going to bring him in for questioning."

"Can I—"

"No!" he barked.

"But—"

"No. No. *No.* Period. End of discussion."

I smiled and nodded my head. "Okay. Fine."

## Chapter Sixteen

It was nearly midnight by the time I returned to the marina. I let myself through the dock gate and rubbed my tired neck as I stumbled down the wooden walkway to the *Plan C*. Two of the overhead lights that generally lit the area between my boat and the main dock were burned out. I made a mental note to let someone know about it in the morning. I thought it was strange that two would have burned out at the same time, but I was exhausted, and the curiosity fled my mind as quickly as it had appeared.

The darkness made it difficult to judge the edge of the dock and the railing of my boat. I rummaged through my purse for the small penlight I kept, and hoped the battery was still good.

He moved with the quiet speed and agility of a cat, never making a sound. I didn't hear him coming. The only warning I had was a scent in the air—some expensive aftershave I'd smelled before, but couldn't place where. I didn't think twice about it when I first noticed it, until I felt his

165

strong arms grab me. One arm firmly around my head, with his hand over my mouth, kept me from screaming out— but I could smell the cologne on him. He wrapped his other arm firmly around my upper body, restricting my arms so I couldn't use them to fight back. I struggled with all my energy, but he was too powerful. I tried stomping on his feet, but he was dragging me backward quickly, away from the rail of the *Plan C*. I couldn't anticipate the location of his feet. He kept me off-balance and unable to stand on my own.

The small noises I was able to produce from under his strong grip disappeared in the air. There was no hope of anyone hearing my struggle. From what I could tell, we were headed toward the end of the dock. I finally managed to get one well-placed jab to one of his feet, and he cursed at me under his breath, but not loud enough to wake any of the few residents who might be snoozing away on their floating homes.

He stopped dragging me once we reached the end of the dock. I relaxed for a moment, hoping to lull him into a false sense that I'd given up. He didn't ease his grip, as I'd hoped. We stood there for a moment, then he reached down to pick up something from the dock, forcing me to bend over with his body. In the instant that he released his hand from my mouth to pick up the end of the coiled rope, I let out the loudest, most blood-curdling scream I could.

"Shut up!" he hissed.

I kept on screaming. He fumbled for a moment with the rope, then draped it over my head, pulling it tight around my neck. Before I could draw a breath for another scream, he kicked the cement block that was tied to the other end of the rope off the edge of the dock and shoved me into the water.

*I'm going to die*, I thought, as I was pulled downward in the dark water. The rope was tight around my neck. I fought against it, but that just made it tighter. I couldn't remember how deep the water was here. The heavy block seemed to drag me down farther and farther. Was it ever going to stop? I tried to pull the rope loose with my fingers. I was running out of air. My life began to flash before me, but I had no time for that. I shoved the adolescent memories of prom nights and first dates out of my head and tried to recall the more important ones—the ones that could save my life.

A swimmer caught in the vortex at the bottom of a spillway would drown trying to fight the irresistible force of the current holding him in the churning waters. I remembered seeing this demonstrated on one of those real-life rescue shows on television. The experts concluded the only way out would be to go with the flow, let it take you down. Once out of its grip, the swimmer could escape to calmer water and resurface. I kicked my feet and pushed my body further down, closer to the ocean floor. This action allowed slack in the rope. I pulled the noose from around my neck and began my ascent toward the surface.

I gasped for air and floundered about in the water, grasping for any part of the dock that would allow me to climb back up. I could hear the clatter of footsteps rushing down the dock toward me. I halted my thrashing and tried to be quiet, in case it was my attacker returning for another opportunity to exterminate me.

"I say! Who's there?" the voice demanded.

I breathed a sigh of relief. "Mr. Cartwright? Is that you?" I called out.

"Miss Lace? Is that you? I heard your screams. What in the world are you doing in the water?"

"Help me out, and I'll tell you," I said, still trying to find a piece of wood that wasn't slimy and slippery.

Sam sat on the edge of a sofa in the main salon of the *Plan C* and scribbled in his notebook as I dried my hair with a towel and recounted the whole terrifying episode to him. Mr. Cartwright had slept through most of the attack, so couldn't offer much help. He did, however, see headlights speeding out of the parking area after he heard my screams, but didn't see the vehicle well enough to give a description.

"I'm telling you, Sam, send a car over to Bradley Parker's house. I'll bet you a hundred bucks he's not there," I insisted.

Sam shook his head and continued writing.

"Are you listening to me? The longer you wait, the less chance we have of catching him," I continued.

"We?"

"We. You. Me. Whoever. Bottom line is, someone tried to kill me tonight. The trail's getting cold. Am I the only one who sees the urgency here?"

Sam scribbled one more word on his notebook, pressing so hard the pencil lead snapped off and rolled to the floor. " 'The trail's getting cold?' Did you learn that from watching old *Bonanza* reruns?"

I glared at him. "What do you think? I made this up? You think I just walked to the end of the dock, screamed my head off, then jumped in? These rope burns on my neck are self-inflicted?"

"You do seem to have it in for Bradley Parker. You're clever enough to come up with this scheme. I'm just not sure you're that conniving."

Another officer entered the *Plan C*, carrying a coil of waterlogged rope with a cinderblock tied to one end. "Our diver brought this up from the area where she says she was attacked," he informed Sam.

I smirked at Sam. "Look how clever I am. I don't miss any details."

Sam ignored this. "Tag it and put it in an evidence bag," he instructed the officer.

"Right," he replied, turning to leave. The officer stopped and turned. "Oh. Charlie radioed. They picked up Parker. He's at the station now."

I gawked at Sam.

"I know. He called me on my cell phone. Thanks, Mac."

Officer Mac left the room. I felt steam building up under my skin. "You already picked up Parker?"

"Yes," Sam admitted.

"And you chose to keep this from me because—?"

Sam scratched his head in thought. "I guess it's because you're so darn cute when your face turns all red, like it is now. And that smoke coming out of your ears reminds me of my last trip to Hawaii, when I got to see a volcano erupt. And when your eyes flash like they are now, sort of like when you disturb an angry mother bear, I just get goose bumps."

I wadded up the damp towel in my hand and flung it as hard as I could across the room, hitting him square in the head.

He laughed. "Are you sure you want to marry that Craig

fellow? What say you and I run off to Vegas and get hitched."

"Yeah. Right. There'd be no survivors in that episode. We'd kill each other before we got across the border."

"Is that a yes?" he asked.

"No. That's a no. Let's go down to the station. I want to watch you question Parker. Get your stuff together," I ordered.

"I love it when you assert yourself," Sam quipped.

"You're weird," I said as he followed me out through the hatch to the deck. It occurred to me that our relationship had evolved from something that provoked nothing but anger and frustration into something very nearly resembling friendship.

Sam held the dock gate open for me. "Ride with me?" he asked.

"No. I'll follow you. It's late. I don't want you to have to bring me back home." We continued walking toward the parking lot.

"Sure?"

"Yeah." I still had a question. "One thing. Why'd you pick up Parker? If he was home, then chances are he wasn't the one who attacked me."

"Ah. That's where you're wrong, and why I make the big bucks. You see, he was home, but I told Charlie to feel the hood of his car. It was warm. He'd been out and had only just returned."

I smiled. "Wow. You're good. Just like Columbo."

Sam puffed up and strutted ahead of me to his car. "That's me. Columbo. Oh, just one more thing, ma'am. If you change your mind about the marriage proposal, I'm totally free. All that talk about Mrs. Columbo? All a ruse. There's no Mrs. Columbo."

I laughed and climbed into the Explorer. "I'll see you downtown," I said, closing my door and cranking the engine.

Bradley Parker was furious. I watched from the dark side of the two-way mirror as he fumed in the interrogation room. Sam sat across from him, pencil in hand and notebook opened flat on the table.

"Where were you tonight, Mr. Parker?" Sam asked.

"I told you. I went for a drive. I couldn't sleep," Bradley Parker insisted.

"You often get up and go for a drive at midnight?"

"As a matter of fact, I do. I've had trouble sleeping lately."

"Why is that?" Sam asked.

Parker was silent.

"Lonely?" Sam continued. He tapped the end of his pencil on the table, studying Parker's response.

"Maybe. No law against that."

"There is if you killed the only person who kept you company."

Parker slammed his fists on the table. "I told you! I didn't kill anyone! You people are crazy!"

"Where is Pamela?"

"Florida. With her aunt," Parker grumbled.

"Guess what. We can't find any record of Pamela having an aunt in Florida. We can't find a record of Pamela having an aunt anywhere. Try again, Mr. Parker."

Parker squeezed his eyes shut. "She told me she was

going to stay with her Aunt Lori in Fort Lauderdale. I swear it."

"Did Aunt Lori have a last name?" Sam asked.

"I'm sure she does, I just don't know what it is."

Sam shook his head. "Think hard, Mr. Parker. Did Pamela give you any other information that could help you out of this difficult situation?"

"No! No! No! She left me! That's all I know. She said I was a horrible person and she never wanted to see me again. I dropped her off at the airport and watched her fly right out of my life."

"Are you a horrible person?" Sam asked.

"Yes! I admit it. Okay? She came over to surprise me with a gift she'd made and found me in a somewhat awkward position with my receptionist. Is that horrible enough for you?"

A picture of Mandy, the big-haired redhead, flashed through my mind.

Sam nodded his head. "I'd say it's a wonder we're not dragging *your* body out of the water with a rope around your neck."

Parker stared at his hands, folded on the table. He didn't say any more. Sam shoved his chair out from the table and stood up. "If you think of anything that might help, let me know."

Sam left Parker sitting at the table. I watched as Sam left the room, and Parker began to sob.

I followed Sam down the hall to his office. "What's next?" I asked.

"We have to charge him or let him go."

"So? Charge him. What's the problem?"

"Can you testify it was Parker who attacked you to-night?"

"You know I can't. But who else could it be? There're no other suspects," I reminded him.

"I know, but it's thin. Lack of other suspects isn't enough."

I gripped the edge of Sam's desk. "I don't believe this. You're going to let him go, aren't you?"

"No. Not tonight, anyway. We're going to hold him as long as we can, but his lawyer will be here in the morning, screaming bloody murder."

I hoisted my purse higher on my shoulder and marched to the door. "I'm going home. I guess I'd better find some sort of protection for myself—maybe a big, mean dog." I stepped through the door. "Or a gun," I continued, closing the door behind me.

I had parked the Explorer in the underground parking garage next to the station. The dimly lit structure was nearly empty at this hour, with only a few cars occupying the spaces. I dug through my purse for my keys as I walked across the expanse of concrete toward the section I thought I parked in. A voice startled me and I stopped short, turning to see where it came from.

"Hello, Devonie. How are you? I heard about your awful ordeal tonight," he said, looking as concerned as a worried father.

I was relieved to see the familiar face. My nerves had been on edge ever since the attack. I relaxed and breathed again. "Garrett. What are you doing here at this hour?"

"I got a call from the night desk at the paper. We keep someone posted at the police station just in case any big stories break. When the call came in that there was trouble at your place, someone remembered you'd been in to see me a couple of times and thought I'd want to know. I tried to call the station, but they wouldn't tell me anything, so here I am. Are you all right?"

"I'm fine. Just a little scared. They're holding Bradley Parker."

Garrett's face lit with amusement. "Did he do it? Attack you, I mean?"

"I don't know for sure. He doesn't have an alibi."

"You and I both know he's as guilty as sin. Poor Diane. It's about time he got what's coming to him."

I nodded in agreement.

Garrett took a step closer. I eyed him. Something was strange. Yet familiar. I looked past him, at the vehicle parked in the slot behind him. The engine was still ticking from the heat. It was a Humvee. Garrett's Humvee. It had to be his. No one else was around. I'd seen it before, but not at the *Tribune*. It was during those hours and hours of viewing the Caltrans videos of traffic around Ralph Campbell's house. That Hummer showed up on a regular basis. I was sure of it. The vanity plates were a dead giveaway. *TRIB MAN*. I don't know why I didn't make the connection while I watched the Caltrans videos. I noticed the size of the vehicle. It was very big—big enough to push a smaller SUV into the path of an oncoming train.

Garrett took another step closer. The scent hit me. His cologne. It was Garrett who'd attacked me tonight. It was Garrett who'd tried to kill me on the railroad tracks. In that instant, I realized it must have been Garrett who'd killed Diane Parker.

I took a step backward. He advanced. I turned to run.

He made a leap for me, catching me by my shirttail. I swung my arms, hitting him squarely in the face with my fists. He ducked and lost his grip on the fabric of my shirt. I blasted past him and raced toward section E. My eyes scanned the garage for the Explorer. I knew it had to be close—just around the next corner. I could hear Garrett's pounding feet on the cold cement. He was close and getting closer.

The sound of his feet hitting the ground stopped momentarily. I ducked behind an old Chevy pickup and turned to see what he was up to. He pulled a gun from under his jacket. I spotted a tire-iron in the back of the pickup and grabbed it. Garrett fired at me. I ducked again and watched his feet from under the pickup. He headed in my direction. I waited until he was close enough that I felt I couldn't miss. At just the right moment, I screamed, stood up, and flung the tire-iron at him. He had his gun raised to shoot. The tire-iron hit his wrist. The gun went off before flying out of his hand and skidding across the cement floor. It slid to the edge of the floor and fell to the next lower level.

I darted out from behind the pickup and raced away from him. Holding his injured wrist, he started after me. There was the Explorer, just as I rounded the next corner. I had my keys in my hand, ready to plunge into the door lock, but Garrett was too close. I'd never have time to unlock the door and get safely in before he caught me. I made a daring move. Daring, because he wouldn't expect it. Surprise. It was all I could think of. I stopped, turned, and ran directly at him. He was moving toward me full blast. As we collided, I ducked and he sailed right over me, landing flat on his back.

I didn't have time to recover from the collision. I lunged

at the Explorer, fumbled to get the right key from the collection in my hand, dropped them, cursed, then finally opened the door. Garrett had just gotten to his feet and was within a couple of yards when I jumped inside, shut the door, and slammed my hand down on the door lock. He banged his fist on the driver-side window as I slid the key in the ignition and turned it. The engine didn't fire immediately. I pleaded with it. Garrett banged harder. He wrapped his jacket around his arm and was doing his best to break the glass.

The engine finally turned over and I jammed it into gear. The tires smoked and burned as I peeled out of the slot, knocking Garrett out of the way. I spotted the lighted exit sign but I was going the wrong direction. I'd have to get turned around to get out of the garage.

Garrett jumped over a railing and suddenly he was in front of me. There was the gun, on the ground. He dove for it, falling flat on his stomach in front of me. I slammed on the brakes. The Explorer skidded to a stop. I watched him crawl toward the gun. I had to get turned around. I shoved my foot down hard on the clutch and grabbed the gearshift. Garrett inched closer to the gun. I shoved as hard as I could. The gearshift would not budge. There was no reverse left in the Explorer. Garrett's fingers nearly touched the barrel of the gun.

My mind flashed back to midnight on the dock. I remembered the noose he'd put around my neck. I recalled the heavy weight of the block, pulling me down to the ocean floor. I thought of Diane Parker, landing on the rocks at the base of the Sunset Cliffs. I put the Explorer in first gear and pressed on the gas pedal. He was so intent on getting his hand on that gun that he didn't realize what was coming until it was too late for him to get out of the way. I rolled the front tire over his outstretched fingers as they reached for the gun. I knew when I'd hit the right spot by the sound of his screams. Then I set the brake and cut the engine.

Caught like an animal in a trap, he couldn't escape. I double checked the brake and eased myself out of the driver's seat. He was bawling like a newly branded calf.

I cautiously stepped around the front of the Explorer and kicked the gun out of his reach. "Bet you were surprised to see me still breathing, huh, Garrett?"

He continued to cry in pain. "Get this thing off me!"

"So you can have a third chance to commit murder? I don't think so," I said, picking up the gun. I moved away from Garrett and sat down on a concrete curb, watching him all the while. "It's starting to come together for me. Tell me if I have it right. Ralph Campbell said he went to the paper with his story about the plutonium, but he didn't talk to Diane, did he?"

Garrett's hand remained pinned under the Explorer's tire. Sweat dripped from his forehead. He finally quit struggling. There was no way he'd wiggle out. "No," he grumbled.

"No. I didn't think so. He talked to you. He wanted to do the right thing, but you had other plans."

"Get this thing off me," he whimpered.

"In a minute. First, I have to see if I've got all the pieces to the puzzle. You convinced Ralph that being a plutonium entrepreneur was far better than a whistle-blower."

Garrett pressed his forehead to the cool cement and rolled it back and forth. He spoke into the floor so I could barely hear him. "Campbell was no angel. I didn't have to do much convincing."

"I'm sure you didn't. Greed is a powerful force." I set the gun on the ground at my feet, feeling secure enough that he couldn't escape and try to hurt me, again. "But I'm still a little unclear how Diane got mixed up in it. Did she discover your little business? Was she going to expose you?"

Garrett raised his head and looked at me. The mention of Diane's name seemed to have a calming effect on him, like music soothing the savage beast. "You know, it was just dumb luck. I'm really sorry it turned out the way it did. I would have won her over, given enough time. She'd have been a great catch—smart, beautiful, ambitious. I hated to have to—"

"You were in love with her?"

Garret laid his head back down. "Get this thing off me before I pass out!" he demanded.

"You were in love with her, but she didn't give you the time of day. I think Diane had too much character to even consider getting mixed up in your scheme. I think you probably knew that, too. She must have stumbled on one of your deals out jogging that morning. If you thought even for a moment that she'd return your feelings, you'd have spared her. Is that it?"

Garrett's eyes began to tear. "She would have loved me, if that jerk of a husband hadn't messed up her head. I almost had her, in the beginning, but she put the breaks on. She had a change of heart. Said she needed time to *find* herself."

I thought about what he said. I had no sympathy for Garrett. He was the lowest form of life still technically considered human. I continued with my hypothesis. "It was you in your Hummer that night at the railroad tracks. You had already planned to kill Ralph, but when you saw me there, you decided to kill two birds with one stone, so to speak. It's all getting clear," I said. "You followed me. I bet you felt like you hit the jackpot when you saw that train barreling down the tracks. Your lucky day."

"Not that lucky."

"No. I guess not. But you did manage to get Ralph out of the way. He was going to talk, wasn't he? I could sense it. I'm sure you could, too."

"Campbell was an idiot. He couldn't see how good he had it."

I scratched my head. "But what about me? Why come after me? As far as you knew, Sam was going after Bradley Parker for Diane's murder. Your little informant down at the police station would have told you that," I said. Then it occurred to me. "Ah. Your informant. He probably filled you in about my session with the Caltrans videos. Vanity plates on a Hummer. Stands out like a Great Dane in a pack of weenie dogs—and all recorded on videotape."

Garrett took in a deep breath. "Get me out from under here or I swear I'll—"

"You'll what? Kill me? You had your chance," I said. "So you figured I'd make the connection with you and Ralph Campbell as soon as I realized you're the Trib Man. If my guess is right, you made a plutonium pickup at his house at least every week," I continued.

Sam and a half-dozen other officers came blasting around the corner, guns drawn. "Devonie! You okay?" Sam hollered. "Someone called in that there were shots fired in the parking garage."

"I'm fine, but he might need a little medical attention," I said, pointing at Garrett.

Sam came to my side. He looked at Garrett, trapped under my tire, then at me. "He's the one?" he asked.

I nodded. "He's the one. When he found out he'd failed tonight at the marina, he came back for another try."

Garrett banged his free hand on the ground. "Get this thing off me before I pass out!"

Sam picked up the gun and handed it to one of the other officers. "Settle down. We'll have this vehicle removed from your hand long before you'll have time to chew it off. In the mean time, why don't you do us all a favor and shut up. You're giving me a headache."

"This is cruel and inhumane. I'll sue you for all you've got. And I'll win. You know I will," Garrett threatened.

Sam chuckled. He draped his arm over my shoulder and walked me toward the exit. "Come on. I'll give you a lift home. Looks like we're gonna need your vehicle for a little while longer."

I was coming down from the adrenaline rush, and my entire body shook. "Okay, but can I make a call first?"

Sam stopped and looked at me. "Craig?" he asked.

I nodded. "I need to talk to him."

"At this hour?"

"He won't mind. It has occurred to me that if the situation were reversed, I'd want him to call me. I've spent so many years alone, I never knew what it meant to really care. Now I do."

## Chapter Seventeen

I arrived forty-five minutes early to meet Pamela's plane. I didn't want to be late. I remembered the first time I'd flown anywhere after suffering a broken heart and having no one at the airport to meet me. It was the first time in my entire life there was no familiar, smiling face at the gate, anxious to know all about where I'd been and how my trip was. I wandered through the crowd of strangers, all there to greet someone else. No one there for me. No one of my own. No one happy to see me. No one. It was the moment that defined loneliness for me. There have been plenty of empty arrivals since then, but the first time was the absolute worst. I didn't want that for Pamela. Not if I could help it.

I spotted her anxious face coming up the jetway. I saw her searching expression, looking for something solid to hold on to. I raised my arm and waved to catch her eye. She spotted me and a smile of relief came over her face. She hurried through the crowd and I opened my arms to hug her. Tears flowed from her eyes. "Oh, Devonie. I'm so sorry I didn't call to let you know where I was. I was just so upset. I wasn't thinking straight," she blubbered.

I patted her back, still hugging her. "It's okay. Everything is fine now. You're okay, and that's all that matters."

I let her go and retrieved a package of tissues from my purse. "Here. Looks like you need these more than I do."

She sniffed and took them from me. "Thanks." Red, puffy eyelids framed her blue eyes. Clearly, she'd been crying for most of her trip across the country. She'd probably be crying even more in the days and weeks to come.

I looked at her small carry-on bag. "Let's go get your luggage."

After getting Pamela checked into her hotel, I bought her dinner and took her to a newly released comedy playing downtown. I was determined not to leave her alone until she was so tired she couldn't have energy to do anything but fall asleep. I hoped she would be able to sleep better than she was able to eat. She barely touched her dinner, and she looked as though she'd lost about ten pounds since the last time I'd seen her. I was exhausted, but I knew how she felt, and there was nothing I could do to make things better for her except to be there with a shoulder for crying on. Tomorrow would be a big day for me, but I'd manage, somehow.

I asked Pamela about her Aunt Lori. She explained that Lori wasn't her real aunt, but she had been a close friend of Pamela's mother—like a sister. Pamela had called her Aunt Lori ever since she was a little girl. Aunt Lori and her husband retired to Florida and offered to help Pamela get back on her feet after Bradley knocked the wind out of her sails. They were financially well off and had a small guesthouse she could live in, rent-free, while she attended culinary school. She'd always dreamed of becoming a world-class chef, but the demands of everyday life kept her from pursuing her dream—until now.

At one-thirty in the morning, Pamela and I were watching *Ever After* on the television in her hotel room. I had tears running down my face when Prince Henry arrived to rescue Danielle from the horrible man who had enslaved her. I glanced over at the queen-size bed on the other side of the nightstand to find Pamela fast asleep. That was my cue to leave. If I didn't get enough sleep, I'd have dark circles under my eyes for the biggest day of my life. I took a mental inventory of the contents of my makeup case, better known as my tackle-box, to recall if I had any concealer.

I left a note stuck to the bathroom mirror that my Aunt Arlene would be by in the morning to pick her up and keep her occupied all day. I switched the lights off and let myself out of her room.

Enchanted. That's the best word I can use to describe how Los Willows looked when I gazed across the lake at the fairytale gazebo, covered with tiny white lights. I stepped into the chauffeured boat that would glide across the lake, delivering me to the other side, and prayed I wouldn't fall into the drink. *America's Funniest Home Videos* flashed through my mind. All those horrible wedding disasters, captured on video for the whole world to see. There was Jason in the front row with his video camera. I was sure he had the same thought in his mind. If only I'd sail over the edge of the boat, he could be in line for the fifteen-thousand-dollar grand prize. I know he was praying for a slippery step or a loose heel on my shoe.

No such luck for Jason. I settled myself on the satin-covered seat and smoothed the front of my beautiful dress. I leaned back in the seat and felt the row of tiny buttons pressing ever so gently into my back. The afternoon held all the promise of a day in paradise. The sun shone warm on the green grass. Birds chirped in the shade trees surrounding the lake. Azaleas bloomed along the water's edge. The scent of honeysuckle wafted around my head, and I glanced around, searching for the source of the wonderful smell. Bougainvilleas climbed along redwood arbors surrounding an area that would be used later for dining and toasting the happy couple, then for dancing into the wee hours.

The little boat arrived at the other side of the lake without incident. Jason filmed with all the zeal of a Las Vegas gambler hoping for the wheels to hit seven-seven-seven, never letting his finger off the RECORD button. I stood up and my attendant took me firmly by the arm to help me disembark. I put one foot on the edge of the boat, smiled at Jason and feigned losing my balance. I knew it would jump-start his heart. I winked at him as I steadied myself and stepped off the boat.

I held my bouquet of pink and white roses and baby's breath and listened to the music as I started up the walk toward the gazebo. Uncle Doug, Aunt Arlene, and Pamela smiled at me as I passed. Sam gave me a thumbs-up as I passed his row. I let one hand loose from the bouquet and returned the gesture. All my closest friends and family were there to share this once-in-a-lifetime event. I tried to see everyone's face, to acknowledge their presence.

Then our eyes met. It was like the first time I'd seen him. Like a dream. That handsome face. That warm smile. Those perfect eyes. I stopped for a fraction of a second and my heart felt like it skipped a beat. I felt goose bumps rise on my arms. But then, in an instant, I felt warm all over. I took another step and returned his smile. At that moment, I knew I'd never know loneliness again. I'd never step off the plane without his smiling face there to greet me, happy to see me, ready to take me to my home—to our home.